LOVE'S PROPHECY

LOVE'S MAGIC BOOK 6

BETTY MCLAIN

This book is dedicated to all who search for a chance of love. To those who keep the faith and never give up on their dreams of love.

CHAPTER 1

*M*addie and her roommate June strolled through the streets, enjoying the fair, eating cotton candy and trying their luck at a couple of games. June won a bear at ring toss. Maddie won some oversized glasses at the sharpshooting booth. The fair was set up close to their university. They were halfway through their senior years and were glad for a chance to wander around and get their minds off testing for a while.

They spotted a fortune telling booth ahead, so the girls headed that way. June was reluctant, but Maddie was wondering if the fortune teller could give her some insight into her situation with Liam. She had not seen him in six months. He went skiing with friends at Christmas instead of coming home. It had been four years since she had seen Liam in the magic mirror. They both had been away at different universities. They did not get many chances to see each other.

When he was on break, he went home to Morristown. When she was on break, she was expected to go home to Rolling Fork. Sometimes, she visited with Dora and Rafe, her sister and Liam's brother, but Liam was not always there when she visited. She made up her mind to look in the mirror again next time she was home. She had not told any of her friends at college about seeing Liam in the mirror because she did not think they would believe her.

They reached the fortune teller's booth and went inside. The fortune teller was made up like a gypsy. She watched them as they approached her table.

"Take a chance on the future," she said. "It is always good to know what to expect."

"You go first," Maddie motioned for June to take a seat.

June sat down, hesitantly, and laid her money on the table. The money quickly disappeared and the fortune teller reached for her hand.

"You have a nice long life line." she said.

June glanced at Maddie and grinned.

The fortune teller studied her hand for a few minutes. June watched her anxiously, because the fortune teller was quiet for so long. The fortune teller looked up at June. "You have already had a glimpse of your true love. Do not delay to establish a relationship. You will have to face treachery from your look-alike. She will try to take what is yours. She always wants what is yours. You will win in the end, but you will face unexpected happenings from unexpected directions. Hold strong to your love. True love is worth fighting for. Do not give up on love."

The fortune teller sat back quietly. June rose from the chair and let Maddie have her turn.

Maddie sat down. She laid her money on the table and watched it disappear. She put her hand on the table for the fortune teller to study.

The fortune teller studied her hand and looked at Maddie.

"Your true love is waiting for a sign from you. He wants to

be sure you are ready to make a life with him. Do not wait too long. Let him know you are his. If you do not make your move soon, someone else will try to make him hers."

The girls thanked the fortune teller and left. They did not discuss what she told them until they moved away from her booth.

The girls wandered over to some picnic tables and sat down. June looked at Maddie.

"I don't talk about my twin sister very often. She went to cosmetology school, while I dropped out of the university to take care of Mom. She would not help. She said she was not putting her life on hold. My sister is rather wild. She is the kind of person who always has a male in tow. Anytime she thinks I am interested in anyone, she does her best to turn his attention away from me and toward her.

I don't know why she is like that. It is almost like she hates me. She has always resented me for being born first. I was born at 11:58 pm on June 30th. She was born at 12:04 am on July 1st.

I was named June and she was named July.

When I was in the museum in Denton, I looked in the mirror hanging there. I saw a man in the mirror. I don't know his name or anything about him, but I did not say anything about him to anybody, because I did not want July to hear about him."

June looked at Maddie to see if she believed her.

Maddie smiled at June. "I believe you," she said. "I saw my true love in the mirror at the gallery in Rolling Fork. It was four years ago. He was nineteen, and I was fifteen. My sister convinced me not to say anything until we were both older. I was lucky. My sister married Liam's older brother. They live in Morristown. I get to see him sometimes." Maddie looked troubled.

"According to the fortune teller's prophesy, I have to let him know we are meant to be together or someone else is going to try to get him interested in her,"

"Doesn't he know about you seeing him in the mirror?" asked June.

"No, I didn't tell him. We were both so young, I did not want to put pressure on him when we could not be together," explained Maddie.

"What does your guy look like?" asked Maddie.

"He has dark hair and he looks rugged, but handsome. I only saw him once, but he was dressed in a flannel shirt and black boots."

Maddie looked at her, startled at her description. Maddie took her wallet out of her purse and flipped to some pictures they took the last time she visited Dora. She found a family group of Rafe, Jason, and Liam. Maddie turned the pictures so June could see them.

June looked at the photos and gasped. She turned white and kept gazing at the photo.

Maddie pointed at Rafe. "This is my sister Dora's husband, Rafe. The one on the other end is Liam and the one in the middle is their brother, Jason."

"Jason," whispered June. "He is the man I saw in the mirror. You know him. Tell me about him."

"Well, his last name is Haggerty. They live in Morristown. They have a logging business. Rafe has been in charge since the death of their father and brother. Jason is in charge of the logging crew. Liam is in his last year at his university. They are all nice guys. Jason comes off as gruff sometimes, but he is a softy when it comes to family," Maddie paused for June to absorb what she told her.

Maddie took out her phone and called Dora.

"Hello, Maddie," said Dora. "Are you about ready for a break?"

"Yes, I am. I'm not interrupting class, am I?" asked Maddie.

Dora was teaching third grade in Morristown. She had been a certified teacher for three and a half years, and she loved teaching.

"No, my students are in gym class this period. What are you doing?"

"My roommate, June and I are visiting a street fair. We needed a break. Have you heard from Liam lately?" asked Maddie.

"No, but as far as I know, he will be home on break in a couple of weeks. Why?" asked Dora.

"I think it is time for Liam and me to get serious, before he becomes interested in someone else," Maddie said, firmly. "Would it be alright if June and I come for a visit as soon as we finish our tests?"

"You and your roommate are welcome anytime. We would love to see you," Dora assured her.

"Is Jason in town?" asked Maddie.

"He away delivering a load of logs, but he should be back by the time you get here. Why?" asked Dora.

"No reason. I was just wondering," said Maddie. "We will see you in a couple of weeks. I will let you know when to expect us. Give my love to Rafe and the kids."

"I will. Take care," said Dora.

Maddie hung up the phone and smiled at June.

"Are you ready to meet your true love?" she asked.

June grinned back. "Yes, I am," she said.

Still grinning, Maddie and June headed to martial arts class. They bowed to Professor Yang and suited up. Maddie was so good at demonstrations the professor often asked her help with the other students. Maddie got June interested in martial arts. Now, she loved the class almost as much as Maddie.

Maddie and June paired up and started their practice. They soon had an audience as more and more students stopped and watched them. Professor Yang stood back and watched. He did not try to get the other students to go back to practicing. He knew they would learn a lot just watching these gifted young ladies.

When Maddie and June finished their routine and bowed to each other, the other students clapped for them. Professor Yang encouraged the other students to continue their own class and went to talk to Maddie and June.

"Miss Hawthorn, Miss Mavorn, you are doing this class an honor by being here," he said, bowing slightly.

"The honor is all ours. Thank you for allowing us to be students here," said Maddie.

"We love our classes here," agreed June.

"Do you have plans for after graduation?" asked Professor Yang.

"Yes," said Maddie. 'I am going to see about opening a martial arts school in Morristown." She was also taking classes in business administration so she could manage the business end of the school.

"I see," said the professor thoughtfully. "Why, Morristown? I thought you were from Rolling Fork."

"Yes, I am, but my sister, Dora and brother, Blake have made their homes in Morristown." With Dora living and teaching there, and Blake running his law firm and living in Hawthorn house in Morristown, she hoped her parents would not try to discourage her about her plans. Maddie grinned at June. "Also, my true love lives in Morristown."

"Ah," said Professor Yang. "True love is not to be taken

lightly. It comes to so few. It is to be treasured. When you get your school started, I would be honored to visit and, maybe, do a demonstration there."

Maddie gave him a big smile.

"That would be great. Anytime you want to come we will be honored to have you," she said excitedly.

"Good luck with your endeavors," he said, bowing slightly, as he turned to go.

"Thank you," said Maddie, returning the bow.

She turned to June excitedly.

"I think we just got our first endorsement," she said. June smilingly agreed.

The girls left to return to their dorm room to study. After a bit of studying, Maddie noticed June looking troubled about something. She waited a while to see if June would say what was wrong, but two subjects later, she still had not said a word, so Maddie decided to do a little discreet questioning.

"Is something bothering you?" asked Maddie.

"I was just thinking about the martial arts school in Morristown," said June.

"You do want to join me there, don't you?" asked Maddie.

"Oh, yes, I would love to join you there. It is just going to cost a lot to build and establish a school. I want to pull my weight, but I don't have a lot of money," said June.

"Oh, is that all? I am not worried about funding. I have a large trust fund. My grandfather on my dad's side of the family set up trust funds for my sisters, my brother and myself when we were born. We received more when he died. I just want you with me. I don't have many close friends. We may even be sisters someday. It will be great to have someone with me I can trust and enjoy having around," Maddie paused and looked at June enquiringly.

June gave her a big smile. "It looks like we are going to open a Martial arts school," she said.

Maddie decided to touch base with Liam. She had his number in her phone, but she had never used it. She dialed the number and waited. Just when she thought she wasn't going to get answer, the phone was answered by a female voice.

"Hello," said the female voice.

"Is Liam there?" asked Maddie.

"No, he stepped out for a few minutes. Can I take a message?"

"Just tell him Maddie called," said Maddie.

"Ok," said the voice as she hung up the phone.

The female turned as Liam came in the door. He noticed her holding the phone.

"Did I get a call?" he asked.

"Yes, someone called Maddie. "She just asked me to tell you she called."

Liam looked surprised. He was pleased to have Maddie reaching out to him. He was beginning to think she never would.

"Who is Maddie?" asked the girl.

Liam looked at her as if he had forgotten she was there.

"Maddie is my sister-in-law's sister," he replied.

"Oh, she is family," she said.

"Yes," said Liam happily. "Maddie is my family. Listen, I have to study for the tests I have early tomorrow, so we need to say good night. I'll talk to you later, Leslie."

"Alright," said Leslie, reluctantly leaving. "I will see you tomorrow. Good luck on your tests."

As soon as she was gone, Liam picked up his phone and called Maddie.

"Hello," said Maddie.

"Hi, Maddie, I received a message that you called," said Liam.

"Yes, I did. I wanted to see if you are going to go home when testing ends," said Maddie.

"Yes, I am. I promised Jason I would help out this summer," said Liam.

"Oh," said Maddie. "I was hoping you would help me look around for a good location for my martial arts school."

"You are opening it in Morristown?" asked Liam.

"Yes, my roommate, June, and I are going to be partners. I already called Dora and she is expecting us as soon as we finish our tests," said Maddie.

"I will make time. I would love to help you scout locations," said Liam, with a big smile. "How have you been?" he asked.

"I am doing good. How about you? You ready for school to be over?" asked Maddie.

"Yes, I am ready to get on with life," said Liam.

"Me, too," said Maddie.

"I'll see you, soon," said Liam.

"Yes, soon," whispered Maddie as they each disconnected.

Liam couldn't stop smiling. Maddie had called him. He had to take things slowly. He did not want to spook her. He had been waiting four years for Maddie to be ready for a relationship with him. He did a jig around the room. The time had come. How was he supposed to study when he was so excited? Soon, they would be together, soon.

CHAPTER 2

*J*ason and his crew unloaded several loads of logs at the Denton saw mill. It was a big order, for a client getting ready to build a new home. They needed to be cut into lumber and cured before they could be used, but the saw mill would take care of that.

Jason looked around and called out to his crew to wrap everything up for the day. They still had a good few logs to unload the next day before they could return to Morristown, so everyone was heading to the motel for the night ... after a few drinks at one of the local hangouts.

Jason decided to go along for a drink. He wanted to keep an eye on his crew. He did not want them getting into any trouble. He was sitting quietly, thinking, when some of the guys whistled at some girls entering the room. Jason glanced up and froze. One of the girls looked like the girl he had seen in the mirror.

He smiled, glad his turn had come. He was ready to settle down and quit playing the field. He had been hoping for a sign from the mirror since Dora and Rafe found each other. When he finally saw her, he couldn't believe it, but the reflection was gone too fast to try and talk to her. Still her image stayed with him, and now, she was here!

July saw Jason as soon as she entered. She recognized him from the mirror, the day June saw his reflection at the museum. June had not known she was there, watching her from a nearby display. July only wanted to talk to her, but the mirror caught her attention. She waited for June to leave and went to look at it closer. All she saw was her own face. She read the display description and knew, whoever June saw was meant to be her true love.

July boldly made her way over to him.

"Hi," she said. "My name is July."

"Hi, I'm Jason. Why would anyone name their child July?" asked Jason.

"I was born in July," said July with a shrug.

Jason shook his head. July had her hand on his arm. He didn't feel anything. When Rafe met Dora they couldn't stand not touching. He shook his head. If this was true love, he wanted no part of it. This girl did not feel like his.

July sat down at Jason's table, without an invitation, and started trying to sweet talk him. Jason did not try to get her to leave. He watched her and listened.

The waitress came over to see what July wanted to drink.

"It took you long enough," said July rudely.

She ordered a drink and started trying to sweet talk Jason again. Jason shifted in his chair. This was not the woman of his dreams.

Jason noticed some of his men getting ready to leave, so he threw some money on the table for the drinks and a tip and got up. "It was nice meeting you, July, but my crew is ready to go. I am driving so I have to leave," Jason hurriedly headed for the door. He glanced back when he was at the door and saw July stuff the money in her bra. The waitress was passing by him. He caught her arm and gave her some more money for the drinks and a tip. He left quickly before July could spot him and come after him. Some of his men were stay ing behind. Hopefully they would steer clear of July.

The next morning, Jason's crew unloaded the last of the logs at the saw mill. The two men, who had stayed behind when the rest of the crew left, were sporting hangovers. Jason looked at them and shook his head.

"You guys should have left with the rest of us," he told them.

"Yeah," one of them agreed. "It's not as if it did us any good to stay. The chick only wanted to talk about you."

"What did she want to know?" asked Jason.

"She wanted to know where you lived and if you had a girlfriend," he replied.

"What did you tell her?" asked Jason.

"I told her we all lived in Morristown and you had a different girl every time I saw you," said the crew member, grinning.

Jason laughed with the rest of the crew. He hoped he had heard the last of Miss July. She was bad news.

They arrived back in Morristown by dinner time. They left the big rigs on the job site and everyone left in their own cars and trucks. Jason headed over to Rafe and Dora's.

Rafe had a large house built for his family, on a five-acre plot, close to the family home. He said he wanted to have plenty of room for his growing family. He and Dora were raising his brother's two children. Frank and his wife Sara died in a car crash years before. Dede was now eight years old and Lars just turned ten. Both children adored Rafe and Dora and had been calling them Mom and Dad for almost three years.

Rafe and Dora announced a couple of weeks ago they

were expecting. They were both very excited, as were Dede and Lars.

When Jason arrived at Rafe's, he found Rafe sitting on the front porch. He was in the swing, drinking a glass of iced tea. "How did the delivery go?" Rafe asked.

"It went fine," said Jason. Jason looked over at Rafe. He wanted to ask him about the mirror, but he didn't know where to start.

Rafe looked at Jason. He could tell something was bothering him. "What's wrong?" he asked.

"When you saw Dora in the mirror how did you feel?" asked Jason.

"I felt my heart stutter. I felt like I had been running hard and couldn't catch my breath," Rafe said thoughtfully. "Did you see someone in a mirror?" he asked.

"Yeah, just a brief glimpse, then I ran into the person in Denton. She came over to talk to me. I didn't feel anything for her. She just felt wrong. I don't know how to explain it. Her name was July, and I hope I never run into her again," Jason ended on a firm note.

Rafe looked at him. He gave him a minute to collect himself.

"It is possible the woman in the mirror is not the woman in Denton. They say everyone has a look alike. Maybe your true love is still out there," he looked at Jason and waited for a response.

"It is very discouraging. I really had my hopes up. When I met July, my hopes plummeted," Jason sighed.

"Don't give up. True love is worth the wait. I treasure every moment with Dora and I know she feels the same."

"Alright, I'll think about it. I had better get home. Mom is not going to be happy if supper gets cold. I'll see you later," he said with a wave as he left.

After he was gone, Dora joined Rafe in the porch swing. She snuggled close to him.

"You heard, Jason?" said Rafe.

"Yes, I started to come out, but I heard what he was talking about and decided he might feel better if I didn't." she said.

"What do you think about this woman he met?" he asked.

"I had a call from Maddie today. She wanted to see if it would be alright for her and her roommate to come here when they finish their tests. I told her to come anytime. She and her roommate were always welcome," said Dora.

Rafe looked at her curiously. He wondered at the change of subject.

"Maddie should know she is always welcome," he said. "What does this have to do with Jason?" asked Rafe.

"Well, Maddie asked if Jason was here. I told her he was away, but would be back soon." Dora looked at Rafe. "Maddie's roommate's name is June. Don't you think it is quite a coincidence for Jason to meet a July and Maddie to bring home a June?"

Rafe looked startled. "Twins!" he exclaimed.

"That would be my guess," grinned Dora. "I think it was probably June who Jason saw in the mirror. July is trying to get a step up on her sister. I am only guessing. We should not say anything to Jason until we know for sure."

"I hope you are right," said Rafe giving her a hug.

"Me, too," said Dora.

It was hard the next day for Rafe to keep quiet about Dora's theory. Jason looked so depressed. He started to tell him, but Jason was called out to handle a problem, and when he returned, he looked much better. He seemed to have put it behind him and was facing the future. Rafe decided to wait, just in case they were wrong. He did not want to get Jason's hopes up only to have them dashed again.

∼

Liam was the first to arrive home. As soon as he finished his last test he headed for home. He did not even wait for his grades to be posted. He knew he could get them off the computer later. He was too excited to wait.

He wandered around the house the first day back. He was too excited to sit and wait, but he did not want to miss Maddie if she arrived early.

His mom watched him wander around for a while. She was curious about what had him so stirred up. "Are you going to help Jason and Rafe on the job?" she asked.

"Yes, but first, I am going to help Maddie scout around for a place to open her martial arts school," he replied.

"Maddie called you?" asked Madeline.

He turned and grinned at his mom. "Yes, she finally called me," he said.

Madeline was thoughtful for a minute. "You know Maddie saw you in the mirror!" she exclaimed. "Did Maddie tell you?"

"No, I overheard you and Dora talking about it when they first came here," Liam explained.

"You did not say anything all this time," she said.

"I did not want to push Maddie before she was ready," Liam smiled at his mom. "She called me."

Madeline came over and gave Liam a hug. "I am so proud of you. You are a son to be proud of. There are not many men who would stand back for four years and give their girl the space to grow in. You are a fine young man."

Liam colored and bashfully returned his mom's hug.

"I am only following the guidance of a wonderful mother. There could not be a better guide anywhere. I love you Mom," Liam gave her another hug and then drew back. "You won't tell anyone about me knowing, will you? I want Maddie to tell me in her own time."

"I won't say a word," promised Madeline. "Now sit and I will get you a glass of lemonade."

"Yes, Ma'am," Liam sat at the table and drank his glass of lemonade and he and his mom talked about his classes and grades. There was no more discussion about Maddie.

CHAPTER 3

*M*addie and June made a stop in Rolling Fork to drop off her winter clothes and pick up her summer clothes. Maddie wanted to talk to her parents about her plans to start a school in Morristown. She also wanted to go by the gallery and take another look in the magic mirror.

Maddie let herself into the house with her key. "Hello, anyone here?" she called.

"Maddie." said Lucy, coming out of the living room and giving her a hug. She then turned to June and hugged her, too.

"Welcome, June. I've heard a lot of good things about you from Maddie," she said.

"Thank you for having me, Mrs. Hawthorn," said June. "I've loved having Maddie for a roommate."

"Mom, we are only going to be here for a day or two. I called Dora and invited myself to visit with her," said Maddie. "I want to show June around town before everything closes. So, is it okay for us to dump our suitcases in my room and take off? We will be back in an hour or two."

"Alright, dear, I'll get some food cooking. Your father should be home by the time you get back. You two enjoy yourselves." She waved goodbye and turned toward the kitchen. She would enjoy cooking for her youngest child. It had been awhile. All of her children had grown up, and she missed them, but she was glad they were all doing so well. After all, she had Rena's children close by to spoil. She hurried into the kitchen to see what she could prepare.

Maddie found a good parking spot downtown and parked. She and June got out and walked. Maddie pointed out her favorite stores as they went along. They stopped at the ice cream parlor and purchased an ice cream cone. They ate it as they continued walking.

"The gallery is just ahead," said Maddie, pointing..

They both threw what was left of their cones in a nearby trash can and headed for the gallery. The bell rang as they went inside. Angelica came forward to greet them. Maddie looked at her, surprised.

"Hi, Angelica, I did not know you were expecting," she said.

Angelica smiled. "Hello, Maddie, yes as you can see, I have two more months. I cannot wait to meet my daughter."

"I bet Dr. Steel is excited," she said.

"Yes, he is. So is Moon Walking," she laughed.

"Angelica, this is my roommate and friend, June Mavorn," said Maddie.

"Hello, June, welcome to the gallery," said Angelica.

"Thank you," responded June with a smile.

"What can I help you ladies with today?" asked Angelica.

"I want to show June the mirror," said Maddie with a smile.

"Help yourself," said Angelica waving a hand toward the mirror.

"It is good to see you, Maddie," she said as she waved them on and turned to help another customer.

The girls made their way over to the mirror.

"It looks different than the one in Denton," said June.

They stood in front of the mirror. At first nothing happened. The girls were about to give up, when Jason appeared in the mirror. He appeared to be washing his face and had his eyes closed.

June gasped. "Jason," she whispered.

Jason opened his eyes and stared at the mirror. He looked hard at the image of June in the mirror and frowned. He saw Maddie standing next to her.

"What are you doing with, Maddie, July?" he asked.

"You know my sister, July?" asked June.

"Your sister?" said Jason.

"Yes, I'm not July. I'm June," she said.

Jason gave a big smile. "Are you twins?"

"Yes, how did you meet my sister?" asked June.

"My crew delivered a load of logs to Denton. We stopped for a drink. She and some friends came in while we were there. I'm glad you are not her," said Jason. "She is not what I am looking for in true love."

"How do you know I am?" asked June.

"I can feel it through the mirror," replied Jason. "I know we belong together. When can we meet?" he asked.

"Maddie and I will be in Morristown in a couple of days," replied June.

The mirror started to fade. June touched it with her finger tips. Jason touched his fingers to hers in his mirror. June sighed and turned to Maddie, who was grinning broadly, happy for her friend.

They started to leave when another image appeared in the mirror. Maddie looked in the mirror with a smile. Liam was in front of the mirror in the entrance hall at his home. It looked like he was getting ready to leave.

"Liam," said Maddie.

Liam looked up and smiled.

"Hi, Maddie, where are you?" he asked.

"I'm in Rolling Fork. I have to talk to my parents about living in Morristown. I haven't said anything to them about it, yet. I should be there in a couple of days. I've missed you," she said.

"I've missed you, too," he said. "I can't wait for you to get here."

The mirror faded back to the mirror image of the girls.

Maddie looked at June and smiled. Both girls laughed and hugged each other.

"I take it the mirror was good to you," said Angelica smiling at them.

"The mirror was great to both of us," said Maddie with a big smile.

June nodded her agreement also with a big smile.

"We will see you later," said Maddie as both girls left.

Angelica shook her head and smiled. There went two very happy girls, she thought to herself.

The Judge arrived home as Maddie drove up and parked her car. Maddie went over to give him a hug and to introduce June. The Judge gave Maddie another hug and welcomed June. They all turned and started for the door, where Lucy was smiling, standing with the door open. The Judge hugged and kissed Lucy, and they all went inside.

They all headed for the dining room, where they could smell the delicious aroma coming from the kitchen.

"Oh, you made spaghetti," said Maddie. "My favorite." She said in an aside to June.

"Yes," agreed Lucy. "I also have a salad and strawberry shortcake with lots of whipped cream for dessert."

June laughed at the look of pure bliss on Maddie's face.

"Come and help me get everything on the table while your dad washes his hands."

Maddie and June followed her into the kitchen and started carrying things to the table. Lucy had already set dishes and utensils out. When they had everything out, Maddie started filling glasses from a large pitcher of tea. June took them to the table as Maddie filled them.

They all sat down and said the blessing. It was quiet for a few minutes as they all enjoyed their food.

"Mom, this is so good. No one else can make it like you," said Maddie.

Lucy smiled. She loved taking care of her family.

They had almost finished eating when Maddie decided it was time to tell them her plans. She looked over at the Judge. "Dad, Mom, I saw someone in the mirror," she said.

"Do you know who it is?" asked the Judge calmly.

"Yes, it was Liam. I saw him before when I was fifteen, but I knew we were too young, so I did not say anything about seeing him to anyone, not even Liam. But I went by the gallery today and I saw him again and he saw me and we talked."

"I see," said the Judge with a sigh. "It was very smart of you to wait a while before letting him know."

"You were very brave," said Lucy. "It must have been very hard not letting him know."

"Yes, it was. I was afraid he would be attracted to someone else, but I thought if he did, he wasn't meant for me. So, I waited and gave us both a chance to grow up before saying anything," Maddie looked at her parents. "There is more. I am going to open a school to teach martial arts. I am going to open it in Morristown. Liam is going to help me look for a place this summer. June is going to be my partner."

"What about your classes. Are you going to finish them?" asked the Judge.

"We only have one more semester. We can take most of it online. If we have to go to the university, it will be briefly and we can make quick trips," said Maddie. "Dora and Rafe and their family will be there. Blake is living there, and June will be there with Jason."

"You know Jason?" asked the Judge.

"I saw him in the mirror and talked to him," said June.

The Judge sighed. "That mirror is a confounded nuisance," he said. All three women laughed at his disgruntled words.

"You can't fight fate, love," said Lucy.

"I know," said the Judge.

He looked at Maddie. If you need us we are still here for you, anytime. You also, June, consider yourself part of our family. Anything you need, just let us know," said the Judge.

Lucy came around the table and hugged Maddie and then June.

June smiled. "Thank you all for including me. It has been a long time since I have felt like part of a family. I love the feeling."

"We mean it," said Lucy. "Anytime you need anything, call us."

Maddie and June said goodnight and went upstairs to go through Maddie's closet to decide what to take with them.

The girls spent the next day packing and later, Lucy took them both to get their hair done, insisting on treating them to lunch while they were out. In the evening, they enjoyed spending time with the Judge, but they were anxious to get to Morristown.

Before they said goodnight, Maddie and June told the

Judge goodbye. He would be gone when they left the next morning.

The next morning, they packed the car and turned to hug Lucy. Lucy blinked back her tears as she hugged them and said goodbye.

"Call me and let me know when you arrive," said Lucy.

"We will, don't worry. We will be fine," said Maddie as they waved goodbye.

The girls both gave a huge sigh of relief to finally be on their way.

Dora had told them to go on in and make themselves at home. She told them she was going to be at the school, but would come straight home when class dismissed. Maddie had a key to the front door.

They pulled into the drive and parked. Before they could get out of the car, Liam was at Maddie's door, opening it for her and pulling her out into his arms. He proceeded to give her a very passionate kiss. Maddie put her arms around him and kissed him back. They both had been waiting a long time for this.

June exited the car on her side and was watching them with a smile, when a voice behind her startled her.

"We may as well say hello like them," said Jason. He proceeded to pull June into his arms and say hello very well. June had no trouble saying hello back.

When everyone came up for air, Maddie and June leaned their heads on the guys' chests to rest for a minute.

Maddie looked up at Liam and smiled. "Could we start over and have another hello?" she asked with a smile. They all laughed.

"Anytime," said Liam.

He looked over to see June still being held in Jason's arms.

"You've been holding out on me, Bro," he said. "When did you meet June?"

"When she arrived a few minutes ago," replied Jason.

"They talked through the mirror," explained Maddie.

"Oh," said Liam. "Welcome to the family, June."

"Thank you," said June faintly. She was still leaning against Jason, and he had his arms tightly around her. She did not mind. She liked having his arms around her.

"Alright you guys, help us get our luggage inside," said Maddie. She headed for the trunk of the car, holding tightly to Liam's hand.

Liam and Jason helped unload and carry their luggage inside. As soon as they put the luggage down, Jason reached for June's hand and pulled her close. Liam took Maddie's hand and, leading her over to sit on the sofa, pulled her close in his arms. Jason guided June over to the loveseat and did the same. Neither, Jason or Liam could stand not being close enough to touch. The more touching, the better as far as they were concerned.

They sat talking quietly for a few minutes. They heard the front door open and Dora called out for Maddie. Maddie answered her, and she walked into the living room. She stopped short when she saw Liam and Jason there, snuggled up with June and Maddie. Dora looked startled, as she gave them all a big smile.

"I see you made it okay," she said.

"Yes, Oh I have to call Mom." She took her phone out and dialed her mom.

"Hi, Mom, we made it. We are here in Dora's living room now." said Maddie.

"You girls take care and keep in touch," responded Lucy.

"We will, Mom. Love you." Maddie hung up the phone and got up to give her sister a hug.

They had barely done saying hello, when Rafe came in. He gave Maddie a big hug and smiled at June. He gave Jason a smile.

"I see you have met June," he said.

"Yeah," agreed Jason with a big smile.

The door opened again and Dede and Lars barreled into the room.

"Aunt Maddie," they exclaimed. Both hurried over to give her a hug.

"Lars, you are getting so tall. If you keep this up, you will be the tallest male in the family," Maddie teased.

Lars colored slightly as he hugged his Aunt.

Maddie hugged Dede and pulled back to give her a look over. "If you get any prettier your dad will need a gun to keep the guys away," she said.

Dede gave a huge sigh. "Please don't give him any ideas. He already screening my friends, and I'm only eight. I can't imagine what he will be like when I get to be a teen."

Everyone laughed at this pronouncement from a precocious eight-year-old. All but Rafe.

"I may have to get your mother to teach me some more karate moves, so I can scare them," he told her while trying not to smile at her

Everyone else laughed again. Even Dede smiled at Rafe and went over and hugged him. He hugged her back and looked over her head and smiled at Dora. They both knew Dede had him wrapped around her fingers.

CHAPTER 4

$\mathcal{B}$ack in Denton, July was trying to figure a way she could get to Morristown. She was sure, if she could have more time with Jason, she could make him fall for her. Her problem was she didn't have a lot of spare cash. She made pretty good money, but she also liked to spend her money on clothes and shoes. She also spent a lot of what she made partying.

July could not stand staying home and being bored. She would never understand how June could spend so much time studying. When their mom was sick and June asked if she could help take care of her, she flatly refused. The sickroom was not for her. Just thinking about being around sick people made her shiver. There was no way she was going to get stuck with sickroom duty.

July absentmindedly leafed through a magazine in the hair salon waiting room. As she passed a page, something caught her eye. She turned back to the page and read it again. It was an advertisement about a job opening for a hairdresser. The job was at a salon in Morristown. July started smiling. It was fate. She tore the page out of the magazine, folded it, and put the page into her pocket. She would check on it as soon as she finished work.

The people in the salon were surprised at how cheerful July was for the rest of the day. They kept giving her strange looks. She just smiled and ignored them.

As soon as July arrived home after work, she opened her laptop and looked up the salon offering the job in Morristown. She filled out the online application and sent it in. Now, all she had to do was wait, something she was not good at. She went to fix herself something to eat while she waited.

July smiled to herself as she thought about the look on Jason's face when he saw her in Morristown. He was sure to be surprised. She frowned. Jason had not seemed very enthusiastic about her, but she was sure she could bring him around. She just needed a little more time to work on him.

There was a ting announcing the arrival of a message. July hurried over to her laptop to check it out. It was the salon. They wanted to talk to her on the phone. They asked her to call tomorrow during business hours, between seven and four. July was so excited she danced around the room. She did not have to be at her present job until nine. She would have plenty of time to call first.

July started thinking about her present job. It was a good job and paid well. Maybe she could take a leave of absence instead of quitting. If things did not work out for her in Morristown, she would have a job to return to. Her apartment rent was just paid, so she had a month before it was due again. She smiled. Everything was working out great. It was as if it was meant to be.

First thing the next morning, right after coffee, July placed a call to the number on the message.

"Hello, Dulce's," said a voice

"Hello, this is July Mavorn. I am calling about the job offer. I applied and received an answer saying to call,"

"Yes, Miss Mavorn, hold a minute. I'll put you through to Marcie. She is in charge of hiring."

The call was switched over while July waited. She was tense with anticipation.

"Hello, Miss Mavorn, thanks for getting back to me. I received your application. It looks good. May I ask why you want to move to a job in Morristown?" asked Marcie.

"My sister is moving there and I am friends with the Haggerty's. I thought I would like to be closer to my sister," said July.

"I see," said Marcie. "How soon could you be here?" she asked.

"I've got the job?" asked July.

"Yes," said Marcie. "It will be on a trial basis. We will give it a month to see how it goes."

"Great," said July. "I can be there on Monday."

"We will see you on Monday," responded Marcie. "Goodbye, Miss Mavorn."

"Goodbye," said July.

July decided to talk to the supervisor at her present job on the phone. It would save having to face her and ask for time off. She placed a call to the salon.

"Hello, Sweet Cuts," said Helen.

"Hi, Helen, this is July. I have a family emergency. I need to take the next two months off. I have at least that much time off built up," said July.

"Alright, I wish we had more notice, but it can't be helped. I hope everything goes alright with your family."

"Thanks, Helen, I'll be in touch."

July hung up the phone with a smile of satisfaction. Everything was working out great. Jason would not know what hit him. She rubbed her hands together. She went to sort through her things to decide what to take with her.

In Morristown, after a lingering goodbye on Dora and Rafe's front porch, Liam and Jason left for the night, only after promising to be there first thing the next day to take the girls around to look for sights for their karate school.

Inside, Rafe drew Dora into his arms.

"I can't say anything," he said with a grin. "I still feel the same way about you. I can't keep my hands off of you," he said with a kiss.

"I am so glad," said Dora, when she could draw a breath. "I feel the same way about you." She raised her mouth for another kiss.

"Alright you two," said Maddie with a grin as she and June came inside. "What kind of way is this for an old married couple to act?"

"The best kind of way," responded Rafe, with a smile.

"I agree," said Maddie. "So, if you will excuse us, June and I will say good night and leave you to it."

The girls went upstairs to their rooms, but they were too excited to sleep. Maddie went to June's room and knocked quietly. June opened the door and stood back for her to enter.

"I'm too wound up to relax," said Maddie. "I can't believe I'm finally getting together with Liam."

She wandered over and sat on the stool at the dresser. June sat on the bed and leaned back.

"I know," she said. "I've already pinched myself to be sure I'm not dreaming. From the way it hurt, I would say I am wide awake."

Maddie laughed. "Liam told me he had been looking

around and has several sights in mind for me to look at. I am anxious to get started. I am more anxious to get started on a life with Liam. It has been a long wait."

"Yes, when my mother got over her illness and told me she was remarrying and moving to Australia, I felt so alone. Then, I met my new roommate and I knew everything was going to be alright. Your family has made me feel so welcome, and Jason takes my breath away. I never thought I would be so happy," said June.

"You are the only one I want to be a partner with. You are never alone. We are here for you and Jason can hardly stand to let you out of his sight. Everything is working out great. We both have found our true loves and we are going to do great in our new school. I had better go and let you get some sleep," said Maddie rising. "Good night, I'll see you in the morning."

June walked her to the door and gave her a hug.

"Good night," she said.

As Maddie left, she heard June's phone ringing. She smiled. Jason was not having any luck sleeping, either.

When Maddie entered her room, she was just in time to answer her ringing phone. She hurried to answer before anyone else was awakened.

"Hi, Liam," she said.

"How did you know it was me?" he asked.

"Your name was on the screen," she said with a grin.

"Oh, yeah, I forgot. I just wanted to say good night one more time," he whispered.

"Why are you whispering?" asked Maddie.

"I don't want to wake anyone up. I just needed to touch base with you again. I have waited so long to have the right to be with you. I have no intention of letting anyone else interfere. I love you, Maddie. You are my light at the end of the tunnel. You are my reason for being. Without you, I am nothing," Liam paused.

Maddie had silent tears rolling down her cheeks.

"Liam, that was so beautiful," she sniffed. "I love you, too. The wait has been very hard, but we can be together now. I have already told my parents about us. They are okay with it. Your mom is a sweetheart. We just have a few minor details to work out, then, we can be together."

"Maddie, don't cry. This is a happy time. I wish I was close enough to hold you," replied Liam.

"I am happy. These are happy tears. I wish I could be snuggled in your arms, too. I have thought about being in your arms often the last four years," said Maddie.

"I have thought about it, too. Soon we will not have to be apart. I will have the right to hold you all night," said Liam.

"Good night, Love," said Maddie. "I'll see you first thing in the morning."

"Good night, dream of me. I'll meet you there," said Liam.

Maddie hung up the phone and turned on the bed and hugged her pillow.

"You know, pillow," she said. "You are a poor substitute for Liam."

Hugging the pillow, she drifted off to sleep.

June was having a similar conversation with Jason. Neither of them wanted to say good night and lose contact with the other. Jason was afraid it would all turn out to be a dream. He could not believe he had found his own true love. He wanted to hold on tightly and never let go. He could hardly believe he had fallen for someone so hard, so fast. June was the one for him. He was so ready to make a life with her.

"I know we don't know each other very well, but I love you and we can get to know all there is to know as we go along," said Jason.

"I love you, too," said June. "We have all the time in the world to learn about each other. All I need to know is that you love me."

"While we are looking at buildings tomorrow, I will take you where I am going to build us a house. I want to be sure you like the location," said Jason. He already surveyed and blocked off five acres of land next to Rafe. He had a crew prepared to start building a house for him. They were getting everything ready to start building. He wanted to have a place to take June when they were married.

"Okay," said June. She was thrilled to know Jason was looking ahead to a life for the two of them.

"Good night, Love," said Jason. "I'll see you in the morning."

"Good night," whispered June.

CHAPTER 5

When the girls stumbled into the kitchen the next morning looking for coffee, they found a large pot already made and waiting for them. Dora and the children were already at school, and Rafe was at work, but Dora left them a note telling them to help themselves to cinnamon buns. They were being kept warm in the oven.

Maddie pulled the plate of cinnamon buns from the oven and, taking her coffee with her, sat at the table and began eating one of the buns. She offered the plate to June, and she and June sat at the table and savored the coffee and the delicious buns. After a few bites, Maddie groaned.

"These are so good," she said.

"Ummm," agreed June.

The doorbell rang and Maddie took her bun with her as she went to answer it. She opened the door to find Liam and Jason standing there. Liam leaned forward and took a bite of her cinnamon bun. He swallowed the bite and then proceeded to kiss her. Jason went around them and headed for the kitchen.

"You taste like cinnamon," said Liam. "I like cinnamon," He proceeded to kiss her again.

Jason found June eating her bun and drinking her coffee. He took the coffee from her and placed it on the table. He lay what was left of the cinnamon bun on the plate. Then, he drew her close and proceeded to say good morning in the best possible way.

When they finished their greeting, Liam and Maddie joined June and Jason in the kitchen.

"Are you girls ready to look at possible school sites?" asked Liam.

"Yes, we are," said Maddie.

"Then, let go," said Jason. They all four grabbed another bun and some napkins before heading for the door.

"We are going in Liam's car," said Jason. "We thought it would be more comfortable than my truck."

Liam opened the door for Maddie to get in the front with him, and Jason opened the back door and held it for June to get into the back with him.

Liam drove first to an abandoned factory building at the edge of town. They all got out and looked around. Liam had the keys, so they went inside as well. Maddie and June looked around. It just didn't strike them as what they were looking for.

"I don't think this is what I'm looking for," said Maddie.

June shook her head. "It just doesn't feel right," she agreed.

Liam smiled and sighed with relief. He hadn't liked the place either, but it was Maddie's decision. He and Jason led them back to the car for the next location. The next stop was on Main Street. It was two buildings down from Blake's law firm. It had, at one time, been a clothing store. Liam took out another key to open the door for them.

"Where did you get all of these keys?" asked Maddie.

"I went by a realtor's office when I arrived in town. I checked out locations and picked up the keys. I thought it would save time," said Liam.

Maddie squeezed his hand. "Yes, it does. Thanks," she said.

"You're welcome," said Liam with a smile.

They all went inside. Liam was holding Maddie's hand and Jason had his arm around June. The girls looked around. There were mirrors on one wall. The front section had a desk and some chairs. They walked further into the building. It was a large open space. It had two dressing rooms and two restrooms. There was a good size room that could be used as an office.

"It needs some work, but I think it will work," said Maddie.

"It has everything we need," agreed June. "I like it, and I like being in the middle of town. It will make it convenient for students."

Maddie looked at Liam. "What do you think?" she asked.

Liam smiled. He liked Maddie asking for his opinion.

"I was hoping you would pick this one. I like it," he said.

"We can get some of our crew to help you get it in order," said Jason.

"Let's go talk to the realtor and see if we can afford it," said Maddie.

"Before we go, let's stop and say hello to Blake. We haven't let him know we are here," said Maddie.

They all went back outside, and Liam locked up. Liam took Maddie's hand and Jason took June's. They decided to walk the short way down to Blake's office.

When they entered the front room of his office, Maddie smiled at the receptionist.

"Hi, I'm Maddie Hawthorn. Is my brother in?"

"Maddie," called Blake as he came through the door to his office. "I thought I heard your voice out here." He came over and gave her a hug.

Blake drew back and smiled when he saw Maddie's hand go back into Liam's.

"When did you get into town?" he asked.

"We arrived last night. This is my roommate, June Mavorn." She said motioning to June.

"Hello, June," said Blake smiling at her.

He looked at her hand firmly in Jason's and smiled again. "I see you have met Jason."

"She saw him in the mirror," said Maddie, "just as I saw Liam."

Blake looked startled for a moment. "It looks like a lot has been going on. Do Mom and Dad know?"

"Yes, I told them before I left for Morristown. They have accepted it." said Maddie. "I also told them I was opening a karate school in Morristown. I have found the place I think will be perfect once it is fixed up. I just need to check on cost."

"Where is it?" asked Blake.

"It is two buildings down from you," said Maddie.

"You mean the old clothing store?" asked Blake.

Maddie nodded. "Yes."

"Come into my office," said Blake. "Let me see what I can find out." They followed Blake into his office and he closed the door. "Have a seat," he beckoned toward the various chairs scattered around.

Maddie sat in one chair and June sat in another. Liam pulled a chair close to Maddie so he could hold her hand. Jason pulled a chair closer to June and reached for her hand. They all waited patiently while Blake started to make a call.

"Hello, Marjorie, this is Blake Hawthorn."

"Hello, Blake, how are you today?" she asked.

"I'm fine. How about yourself? Did you get Lance into little league?" asked Blake.

"Yes, after I talked to the coach, I did not have any more problems."

"Good. The reason I'm calling you today is about the clothing store just down from my office. Is it still available?"

"Yes, the owner called me a couple of days ago. He's willing to take a big cut in price if I can get it off the market for him. Why, do you know someone who might be interested in it?'

"Yes, my sister. She wants to open a karate school. She likes the location, but she said there would have to be a lot of modifications done before it is usable. If the price is right, she might be able to swing it," said Blake.

"Tell her to come and see me. I'll make sure the price is right," declared Marjorie.

"Alright, Marjorie, she's here in my office, now. I'll send her over. Just give me a chance to look over any contracts before anything is signed."

"Okay, send her over," said Marjorie.

Blake hung up the phone and grinned at the group.

"Marjorie is with Decan Realty. You go over and talk to her but don't sign anything until I look it over," Blake instructed Maddie.

Maddie got up and went to give Blake a hug.

"Thanks, Blake, I'll go right over. You guys know where Decan Realty is, don't you?" she asked turning to Liam and Jason.

"Yeah, I would say so, since I have been opening places with their keys," replied Liam. The group laughed at this observation.

They piled back into Liam's car and he drove to Decan

Realty. Inside, Maddie asked to speak to Marjorie. Marjorie came forward to greet them and escorted them back to her office.

"I'm very glad to meet you, Maddie. We are all very fond of Blake. He has been a blessing to our town. He helped several teens to straighten out and he is always ready to help," said Marjorie.

"I'm glad Blake is making a life for himself in Morristown," said Maddie.

"The town is blessed to have him," remarked Marjorie.

"After I talked to Blake, he called back and asked me to include a large storage area in the deal. It goes behind the clothing store and behind the store next to it; I have drawn up the papers with an estimate. I have one set with the storage area and one set without. You can take both sets to Blake and let him look them over and decide which one you are interested in. I have reserved both for you until you decide, so no one will sell them before we hear from you."

"Thank you," said Maddie. She took the papers from Marjorie and left to take them back to Blake. She was wondering why he increased her space.

When they got to Blake's office, they found him waiting for them. He ushered them into his office before they could ask any questions.

Blake held up his hand as Maddie began to speak.

"Before you ask any questions, let me explain a few things."

"Okay," said Maddie.

"I asked Marjorie to include the extra space because it would make an excellent gym to go with your school. People who already know some martial arts may just want a place to work out. It would also be a great place to keep teens busy and out of trouble," he explained.

"I agree, said Maddie. "I just don't know if I can afford the extra right now."

"It won't be a problem," replied Blake. "After you left, I called Dad and Dora. Dad is going to purchase the buildings for you. I'm going to pay for the renovations and Dora is going to pay for whatever you need in the way of furniture for the school and gym," Blake paused to let Maddie catch her breath and speak.

"Why are you all doing this? I have my trust fund. I could pay my way. I might not be able to start out so big, but I could do it more slowly."

"We know you could, but we want to help. You will need your funds for operating expenses for the first year or two, until you get the school running solvent. The only thing we want in return is a lifetime membership in your gym. It will save us money in the long run. This way we won't have to build gyms in our homes. I know Dora misses having a place to work out. We can't always exercise outside. I know I miss my workouts. What do you say? Is it a deal?" Blake waited for her to reply.

Maddie looked at June, who smiled and nodded her head. She looked at Liam. He squeezed her hand.

"Whatever you want, I'm behind you 100 percent," he said.

Maddie turned back to Blake with a big smile.

"You have yourself a deal and soon a new place to work out," she said.

"Good," smiled Blake. "Let me look over these papers and get things rolling."

They got ready to leave. Maddie and June both gave Blake a hug. Jason and Liam shook his hand. When they got outside, Jason was talking quietly to Liam. Maddie wondered what they were up to.

"We need to make one stop before we take you girls out to lunch," said Jason. He was smiling at June and holding tightly to her hand. He looked as if he might be a little nervous.

Jason helped June into the car and entered on the other side, slipping into the seat beside her. Meanwhile, Liam stole a quick kiss from Maddie before helping her to be seated and getting into the driver's seat. Liam drove to the middle of town and parked. They were parked across from a nice restaurant and right beside it was jewelry store. Instead of heading for the restaurant, the guys lead them toward the jewelry store.

Jason led the way, June's hand tucked firmly in his. They went over to the counter. He did not see anything he liked there so he moved on down. A clerk came over to see if she could help. Jason asked to see a tray of engagement rings. June gasped. Jason looked at her and smiled. He then looked back at the rings the Clerk had set on the counter. He looked them over. He glanced back at June. He noticed she was eyeing one particular ring. It looked nice, so he asked the Clerk to let them see the ring.

The Clerk handed him the ring. He took June's hand and tried the ring on her finger. It fit perfectly.

"June Mavorn, will you marry me?" he asked.

June threw her arms around his neck and, with tears running down her cheeks, nodded her head. Jason gave her a kiss then turned and handed his credit card to the Clerk.

While Jason and June were occupied, Liam steered Maddie toward some engagement rings also. He wanted something unique. His Maddie deserved something special. He couldn't find anything to suit him.

"Do you have anything else?" he asked the Clerk.

She looked at him and then disappeared into the back room. She came back a couple of minutes later, setting a tray of antique rings on the counter in front of them. Liam looked at the rings and smiled. This was more like it.

Maddie looked at the rings and gasped. One of the rings stood out to her. It had a bright green emerald in an antique setting. There were small diamonds around it. They were mounted on an antique gold band. She absolutely loved it. She did not notice Liam watching her face. He smiled with satisfaction. He pointed to the ring and the Clerk handed it to him.

He took the ring and held Maddie's hand as he slid it on her finger. Maddie gasped and stared at the ring and then at Liam.

"Maddie Hawthorn will you be my wife?" he asked.

"Yes," she whispered.

He held her close and kissed her. When the kiss ended, he handed the smiling Clerk his credit card.

When all the business was completed, the guys, holding tightly to their ladies, guided them next door for a celebratory luncheon. They were all too busy staring into each other's eyes to even notice what they were eating.

CHAPTER 6

On the way back to Rafe and Dora's Liam pulled into the five-acre lot next to them. There were workers there. They had already done a lot of work on the house and there were even people working on the landscaping.

They all got out of the car, with Jason and Liam hurrying to open June and Maddie's doors.

"I can give you an idea of the rooms and the layout of the house, but it will be a whole lot easier to see in a few days," said Jason.

He pointed out the rooms and guided June around, showing her his vision for their new home. June nodded a few times but did not say much. Jason was beginning to get anxious, thinking maybe she did not like the place.

Finally, he stopped and faced her. "If you don't like it, we can build elsewhere," he said.

June looked at him startled. She smiled into his eyes.

"I think it is absolutely perfect," she said. She put her arms around his neck and kissed him.

Maddie and Liam had wandered away from them. They were looking around and wanted to give the other two a little privacy. As much privacy as you could get it the middle of a building site with workers all around.

As they returned to the other couple, Maddie heard Jason suggest he and June could elope. She did not give June a chance to answer.

"No, absolutely not, you cannot do such a mean thing to your family. Your mom and my mom will plan a double wedding for me and June. I have to see when Dad can get away and I have to check with Bobby to see when he can come."

She saw Liam and Jason beginning to look alarmed and hurried to reassure them.

"It will not be as big as Rafe and Dora's wedding. We will not have to check with Uncle Ralph. I promise we will get it arranged as soon as we can," she looked at Liam pleadingly.

Liam drew her close and drew a long breath. "Do you think Bobby will be able to make it?" he asked.

Maddie smacked him on the chest.

"We are talking about our wedding and all you can think about is seeing Bobby Larroue?"

"Bobby Larroue," said one of the workers. They had been listening to the group with amusement. "You know Bobby Larroue?" he asked.

"Yes," said Maddie. "He is my Godfather."

"Boss," said the worker, turning to Jason. "You are going to invite us to your wedding, aren't you?"

Jason groaned, and Maddie laughed. "Let's wait and see if he is coming," said Jason.

The workers accepted his answer and went back to work. Jason and Liam led the girls back to the car.

"We need to go see your mom," said Maddie once they were all seated and ready to go.

Liam turned the car toward home.

They all trouped into the Haggerty house and Liam called out for his and Jason's mom.

"Well, there is no need to yell. I am right here. Hello, Maddie," she said coming from the living room and heading over to Maddie to give her a hug.

"Hello, Madeline, it is good to see you. This is my friend June," said Maddie.

"Hello, June," said Madeline. She went over and gave June a hug, also.

"Mom," said Jason. "I asked June to marry me and she said yes."

Madeline smiled at June and gave her another hug.

"Welcome to the family, June," she said.

"Maddie and I are also engaged," said Liam.

"That is wonderful. You guys don't mess around, do you?" she said hugging Maddie again.

"We want to have a double wedding here, if it's alright with you," said Maddie.

"I would love to plan a double wedding for all of you," said Madeline, getting a little teary eyed. "How much time are you all going to give me?"

"I have to call my parents and see when my Dad can get away. I know Mom will want to help with the plans. I also have to call Bobby and see when he can make it," said Maddie.

"Come into the living room and we can sit and talk," said Madeline.

They all followed her into the living room. Jason guided June over to the sofa and sat down pulling her close to his side. June smiled up at him and snuggled closer.

Madeline took the recliner and Liam sat on the other end of the sofa and pulled Maddie down into his arms. He gave her a quick kiss on the end of her nose. Maddie smiled up into his eyes. She was so glad they were finally together. It had been a long time to wait for true love.

Meg and Anna came into the room from the kitchen. When they saw Maddie and Liam snuggled up together, they stopped and grinned at Maddie.

"Did Liam finally get around to declaring his intentions?" asked Meg.

"Yes, he did," said Maddie. "I said yes."

She held up her hand for them to see her ring.

"OOOh," squealed Anna as they both rushed over to admire Maddie's ring.

"Not only did Liam declare his intentions, so did Jason. He is engaged to my friend and soon to be business partner. Anna, Meg, meet June," said Maddie motioning to Jason and June.

The girls abandoned Maddie and rushed over to admire June's ring and welcome her to the family.

June found herself surrounded by family. These girls would soon be her sisters. She never felt so much love directed toward her. She smiled at Jason and snuggled closer to him. She felt so loved and safe in his arms.

Jason smiled back at her. He felt like his life was finally coming together, just the way it was supposed to.

"I need to call Mom and Dad," said Maddie. "They need to hear this news from me." Liam let her pull away slightly, but kept his arm around her.

Maddie took her phone out of her pocket and dialed her folks.

Everyone sat back quietly and waited for Maddie to talk to her mother.

"Hello," said Lucy Hawthorn.

"Hi, Mom," said Maddie. "Is Dad there?"

"Yes, he is here we were just about to sit down to eat.

Uncle Ralph dropped by for a visit unexpectedly. How are you and June doing? Your dad told me about you finding a building. Are you ready to move forward with your plans?"

"Yes, Blake is taking care of all of the paperwork for me," replied Maddie. "The reason I am calling is to let you know Liam asked me to marry him and I said yes. Jason asked June and she said yes, also."

"Well, I can't say I'm surprised. You told us before you left you were in love with him. I love you Maddie. I hope you and Liam will be very, very happy. Tell June and Jason congratulations from me and the Judge."

"We want to have the weddings here in Morristown. I told Madeline you would want to help. We are having a double wedding. Ask Dad how he feels about giving away two brides at once," said Maddie.

"You tell Madeline I will call her tomorrow so we can start making plans," said Lucy. "Hold on just a minute. Your Dad just came in with Ralph. I will let you talk to him."

"Hello, Maddie," said the Judge. "How are things in Morristown?"

"Hi, Dad, Morristown is great. June and I are very excited about our school. Thank you for buying the building for us. I really was not expecting you to do that."

"I wanted to help you two girls get started," said the Judge.

"Dad, Liam proposed, and I said yes. June and Jason are engaged, also. How do you feel about giving away two brides at once?" asked Maddie. "We want to have a double wedding,"

"You tell Liam, I am never going to give away my daughter, but I will walk you and June down the aisle to start forward into your new lives."

Maddie had been startled when he had started talking, but by the time he finished, she had tears in her eyes.

"Dad, that was beautiful," she said. "I love you."

"I love you, too, Maddie girl," said the Judge. "Hold on just a minute. Uncle Ralph wants to say hello."

"Hello, Maddie," said Uncle Ralph. "I hear you are about to get married."

"Yes, I am," said Maddie. "It is nice to hear from you, Uncle Ralph."

"How are Dora and Rafe doing?" he asked.

"They are doing great. They are very happy," declared Maddie.

"Did she get the young man and his family straightened out?"

"Yes, Harry and his family are doing very well," Maddie looked at Jason and got a thumb's up.

"Well, Maddie I wish you and your young man the best of luck. Don't forget to send me an invitation to the wedding," said Uncle Ralph.

"I won't forget. Good night Uncle Ralph," said Maddie.

"Maddie," said her mom. "I love you. Don't forget to tell Madeline I will call her tomorrow."

"I won't forget. I love you, too. Good night."

Maddie hung up the phone and turned guiltily toward Jason.

"I'm sorry Jason. I could not say no to Uncle Ralph." She looked at him pleadingly.

Jason drew a long sigh. "It couldn't be helped."

Everybody else, except June, laughed at his disgruntled expression. June had no idea who Uncle Ralph was so she didn't know what the fuss was about. "Who is Uncle Ralph?" she asked Jason.

Jason looked down into her face. He was surprised she did not know about Uncle Ralph. After all, she had been Maddie's roommate. "Maddie and Dora just call him Uncle

Ralph. He is Dora's Godfather. He is also our governor," said Jason.

June sat up quickly. "You mean the Governor is coming to my wedding!" she exclaimed. She turned and looked Jason in the face. "Is it too late to elope?" she asked.

Jason pulled her back into his arms.

"You are not eloping," declared Maddie. "We are going to have a double wedding. Uncle Ralph is a sweetheart. You will hardly notice him being there."

Liam and Jason were chuckling. Madeline, Meg and Anna were smiling. They all remembered the sensation Uncle Ralph's presence caused at Rafe and Dora's wedding. It was not a bad sensation. In fact, they had all enjoyed meeting Uncle Ralph, but, he did travel with security and news people. There was no way for him not to be noticed.

"I feel bad," said Maddie. "I had not even thought about Harry and his family until Uncle Ralph asked about him."

"He is doing fine," said Jason. "Harry's leg is fully healed. Blake helped him get the house next door to Albert and Mary. Ruby, Harry's wife, is doing some light housekeeping and cooking for them. Mostly she just keeps an eye on them. Mary is still helping the children with school lessons and Harry is doing yard work. Lester, Harry's son, helps him when he is out of school. Harry keeps up Dora and Rafe's place. He also takes care of Blake's place. We also have him take care of our place. We keep him pretty busy, but, he really enjoys the work. He likes it lot more than working with the logging crew."

"I'm glad everything worked out for them. They are a great family. Dora has great instincts when it comes to knowing who needs help and who just wants to take advantage," said Maddie.

"Madeline, Mom told me to let you know she will call you tomorrow so the two of you can start planning," said Maddie.

"Okay, I'm sure we can get everything organized," said Madeline.

"What did your dad say about giving the bride away?" asked Liam.

"He said to tell you he was never giving his daughter away, but he would be glad to walk me and June down the aisle to start forward into our new lives," said Maddie. All the ladies wiped away a tear or two at the Judge's words.

"What a beautiful way to express himself," said Madeline.

Jason and Liam pulled their ladies closer to their sides. They understood the Judge's sentiments, but they were looking forward to having their ladies to themselves.

Jason pulled June to her feet. He still held her close to his side as he turned to face his family.

"June and I are going to take another look at our new home. The crew should be gone for the night and we can get a better idea how things are going," he said. "Don't hold dinner. I am taking June out to celebrate our engagement."

Madeline got up to give both June and Jason another hug and they said goodbye and left.

Maddie smiled at Liam. Both of them knew Jason just wanted some alone time with June. They fully understood. They were both trying to think of an excuse they could use to have some time to themselves. Liam smiled back at her and squeezed her closer.

CHAPTER 7

So, this was Morristown. July checked into a bed and breakfast place. It was close to downtown. She thought it would be her best option until she checked out the job at Dulcie's hair salon. It was late when she arrived, so she checked in and decided to look for a place to eat. She did not have to be at the salon until Monday. She had a day to look around and get the lay of the new town.

As she looked around, she spotted a seafood place on the edge of town. Seafood had always been a favorite of hers, so she headed toward the restaurant. There was a nice crowd there, but July did not have to wait for a table. She was seated and the waitress came and took her order. She ordered a seafood platter and sat back to look around and wait for her food.

Blake was at a table across the room from July. He was enjoying his own seafood platter while looking over some papers. The waitress stopped at his table and he lay down his papers while talking to her. She refilled his glass and left. Blake felt someone staring at him and looked around to see who it could be.

When he met July's eyes across the room, he was startled. He wondered what June was doing here by herself, without Maddie or Jason. He supposed he should go over and say hello and find out what was going on. Blake motioned for his waitress. When she came over, he asked her to put the rest of his seafood in a takeout box. He took his drink and headed for July's table.

"Hello, June," he said. "Why are you here all by yourself? Where are Maddie and Jason?"

July looked him over before answering. "You know my sister June?" she asked.

"You are not June?" he asked startled.

"No, I'm July. I just arrived in town. I did not know my sister had arrived here so soon," she said. "Who are you?"

"I'm Blake Hawthorn. My sister Maddie is June's roommate at the university."

Blake put his hand out to shake while he introduced himself.

July put her hand in his. An electric spark passed between the two hands. Both of them drew back, startled.

"I'm sorry," said Blake. "It must be static electricity. Do you mind if I join you?"

"Not at all," said July motioning to the empty chair.

Blake sat in the vacant chair. The waitress came over bringing him his takeout.

"Thanks, Ellie," said Blake.

"You are welcome, Mr. Hawthorn. Can I get you all anything else?" she asked.

Blake looked at July inquiringly. She shook her head.

"No, we are fine, thanks, Ellie," said Blake.

Ellie left and Blake turned his attention back to July.

"Are you planning to help Maddie and June with their school?" asked Blake.

July paused. She had no idea what Blake was talking about. She did not want him to know how ignorant she was about her sister's plans.

"No, I'm a hairdresser. I will be working at Dulcie's Salon," she replied. "I start Monday."

"Dulcie's is a nice place. I have had my hair styled there a few times. They do nice work and are friendly," said Blake. "You'll like it there."

"I'm sure I will," agreed July.

"Are you staying with Maddie and June while you are here?" asked Blake.

"No, I took a room at the bed and breakfast. I wanted to be close to my job. I don't know my way around, yet. I thought I could look around and find a place after I see how the job is going to work out," said July.

July looked at Blake. He was very nice looking. His type usually did not pay any attention to her. She wondered why the electricity between them. She never had it happen to her before. She felt strange around him. She had never felt like this before. She shook her head. What was wrong with her?

Blake looked at July. It was strange about the shock treatment. He hardly knew what to say to her. He never had this problem before. He had always been confident in his dealings with people. He could hardly believe he was feeling so tongue tied around July. He looked at her again and saw her plate was almost empty.

"Would you like a dessert?" he asked. "They have a great lava cake here."

July looked down at her plate. She had not been aware of eating. Somehow, she had cleaned her plate.

"I don't usually eat dessert," she said.

"Come on," said Blake, grinning. "We can share it."

He motioned the waitress over.

"We would like a slice of lava cake with whipped cream on top and two forks," he ordered.

The waitress left with his order and he looked over at July and grinned.

"You are in for a real treat," he said.

July grinned back at him, but did not say anything.

The waitress was back with the cake in just a moment. She placed the cake in the middle of the table and laid the two forks on a napkin.

"Enjoy," she said, smiling as she left.

Blake picked up one of the forks and motioned for July to take the other. He waited for her to take the first bite. He smiled as July took her first bite and closed her eyes to savor it. Then he took his first bite.

"Anything this good is probably illegal," said July.

"I know," agreed Blake. "But it is not listed in any of my law books, so until I hear otherwise, I am going to keep indulging."

"You are a lawyer?" asked July.

"Yes, I have an office just down the street," replied Blake. "I have been practicing for about four years."

"You like being a lawyer?" asked July.

"I love it," said Blake. "Do you like being a hairdresser?"

"Yes, I do. It is something I am good at, something, all my own. While I was growing up, my mom was always telling me to do better. She was always encouraging me to make good grades like June. No matter what I did, she always said June could do it better. Well, hair design is my thing and I do not have to compete with June."

Blake looked at her thoughtfully.

"I did not have to compete when I was growing up. I was

the only boy. I had three sisters and Dad had us all learn self-defense and martial arts. Any one of my sisters could probably beat the crap out of me. But they did not try. We had a lot of friendly competitions, but we loved each other and looked out for each other."

"It sounds like you had a very nice childhood," remarked July wistfully.

"Yes, I did," agreed Blake. He looked down at the plate. They had cleaned it while they had been talking. Blake picked up the check from the table and motioned for July to join him. "Come on, I will give you a lift to the bed and breakfast," he said.

"You don't have to pay my check," said July following him.

Blake took her hand and led her toward the front. The shock from touching was not as bad this time and went away as he kept holding her hand.

"How do you know I need a ride?" asked July with a smile.

"Do you have a ride?" asked Blake, looking at her.

"No, I walked over. I was looking around," said July.

"It has turned night while we were eating, so I will see you to the bed and breakfast," said Blake firmly.

"Okay," agreed July. "Thanks."

They went outside and Blake led the way to his car. He still had July's hand firmly in his. After seating her in the passenger seat, he went around the car and seated himself in the driver's seat. He did not ask her any questions, but drove straight to the bed and breakfast.

When he stopped, he hurried around the car to open the door for her.

"Thanks," said July. "Thanks for the lift, and the cake."

"It was nice meeting you, July," said Blake. "I hope you decide to stay in Morristown."

Blake took her hand and experienced another shock. He looked at July startled. She looked just as startled.

"I have never been shocked like this by touching anyone else," said Blake. "We must have an electric current running between us."

"I guess," agreed July. "It has never happened to me before either."

"Good night, July," said Blake squeezing her hand. "I'll be seeing you."

"Good night, thanks for the ride," said July. She turned and, with a last smile for Blake, went inside.

Blake shook his head and, getting in his car, headed for his home.

Jason drove June back to their new home site. The workers had left for the day, but there was still plenty of light to look around. They were in Jason's truck, and when he stopped in front of the building site, June waited for Jason to come to her side and open the door.

Jason opened the door, put his arms around June and helped her out of the truck. He let her down in front of him and pulled her close in his arms. June put her arms around his neck and held him close as they kissed.

"Ummm," said Jason as he rested his forehead against June. "I am so in love with you. I can hardly wait for us to be together. I am so glad you looked in the mirror and saw me."

"I love you, too. I am glad the mirror showed us our true love. I am also glad the fortune teller at the street fair told me to not waste any time letting you know about us," said June.

Jason grinned. "So, we have a fortune teller's prophesy going for us, too?"

"Yes," said June. "She told both me and Maddie to stop messing around and let our true loves know we were ready before they found someone else. At the time, I did not know who you were. I had only seen you one time, but when Maddie showed me your picture, I knew you were mine."

Jason hugged her close and kissed her again.

"We belong together, for now and always," he said.

"For now and always," agreed June.

He took her hand, and they made a tour of their home. June was so excited. She had never had a home all her own before. Of course, it would be her and Jason's home, but that just made it better.

After Jason was satisfied June had seen everything there was to see in the building site and approved of all his plans, he drove her back to Rafe and Dora's. Liam and Maddie were sitting on the porch in one of the swings. Jason led June to the other swing, seated her beside him and put his arm around her, holding her close.

"So," said Jason. "Were any more plans made after we left?"

"Not really," said Liam. "Mom and Lucy are going to talk tomorrow. I guess they will let us know what is going on after they decide."

Maddie laughed. "It is not as bad as you sound. We can always veto any plans we do not like."

"I don't really care what plans they make as long as they don't make us wait too long," said Liam.

"Yeah," agreed Jason. "I have been waiting a long time for June."

He looked into June's eyes and smiled.

"I am ready to move forward. Standing still is not my style," he said.

June squeezed his hand.

"Mine either," agreed Liam hugging Maddie close and kissing her.

Rafe and Dora came out and joined them. Rafe sat in one of the rockers and pulled Dora down into his lap. Dora settled back against him with a sigh.

"Where are Dede and Lars?" asked Maddie.

"Lars is spending the night with a friend and Dede is up in her room listening to some music," said Dora.

"Have you heard anything else from Blake about your school?" Dora asked Maddie.

"No, he probably won't have any news until Monday," said Maddie. "He seemed to think everything was going to be straight forward. No surprises."

"Good," said Dora.

"Thank you for agreeing to help with the furnishings. Are you sure you can afford it?" asked Maddie "After all you have the baby to think about now.".

Dora smiled. She lay her hands on top of Rafe's where they rested on top of her small baby bump.

"Mom and Madeline are so excited about this baby, I doubt I will have to buy diapers before I start potty training. I told them to wait to see if it is a boy or girl before buying anything else," said Dora.

Everyone laughed at this very true statement.

"I can very well afford a few furnishings for your new school. After all, I am going to be using the gym. I will love having a place to work out. It will be nice to have my sparring partner close by again. I have missed our practice sessions," Dora grinned at Maddie.

"I have missed sparring with you, too," said Maddie.

"I talked to Uncle Ralph earlier. He was visiting Dad when I called. He told me to tell you hello. He also asked about Harry and his family. He told me to send him an invitation to our wedding. I told him I would ... I have to call Bobby tomorrow and see what his schedule is like. I want to check with him before Mom and Madeline start making plans," said Maddie.

"Maybe you will get lucky and Uncle Ralph will not be able to make it. He will be sure to send you a nice gift though," said Dora.

"Jason will breathe a sigh of relief," said Maddie with a laugh.

June squeezed Jason's hand and smiled at him.

"It's okay. I have accepted his possible appearance," said Jason.

"It is not Uncle Ralph," said Dora. "He's a sweetheart. It is all of the people he has to bring with him." Everyone nodded their heads in agreement.

It was quiet for a few minutes as everyone enjoyed the nice night snuggled up with their loved ones.

"Liam, are you going to build yourself a house when Jason gets through with his?" asked Rafe.

"I may wait a while to start building, if it is alright with Maddie," said Liam. "With Maddie getting her new school started and me starting work at the logging camp, we are going to be pretty busy. I thought we could stay with Mom and the girls for a while until we get ready to start building,"

He looked at Maddie inquiringly.

"We will talk to your mom and see if it is okay, but it will be fine with me," said Maddie.

"Well, pick the spot you want and we will mark it and make sure it is yours," said Rafe. "If each of us and Meg and

Anna get five acres each, the home place will still have twenty-five acres."

"Lars and Dede should have five acres each. They should get Frank's share," said Jason.

Liam and Rafe nodded in agreement with him.

"Mom will still have enough for the orchard and a garden, and her chickens, but she will not have too much land to look after," said Liam.

"She will not have to worry," said Rafe. "We will all pitch in and make sure she is alright."

Everyone was nodding their heads in agreement.

"I think I will get down the map of the property and block it off in five-acre plots and get everyone pick their spots," said Rafe.

"Good idea," said Jason. "We can have it all fixed and when each person gets ready to build, they can just go ahead."

"Well, said Rafe, easing Dora up and standing. "We will say good night. We will see you all in church tomorrow."

"Good night, if you girls need anything, Maddie knows where everything is," said Dora.

"Good night," responded Maddie, Liam, June and Jason.

After Rafe and Dora went inside, Liam looked at Maddie.

"I had better let you get some sleep. Do you want me to pick you up for church in the morning?" he asked.

"Yes, please," said Maddie. "I'll walk you to your car."

She walked him over to his car, where she melted into his arms for a good night kiss. She wanted a moment of privacy and she wanted to give Jason and June a moment of privacy, also.

Maddie and Liam kissed and held each other close. When their breathing slowed, Liam gave her another quick kiss and turned her toward the porch.

"Go, I will watch until you get inside," he said.

Maddie gave him a lingering look and headed for the porch. She passed Jason on his way down.

"Good night, Maddie," said Jason with a grin.

"Good night, Jason," said Maddie.

She joined June on the porch. The girls turned and waved at Liam and Jason, then turned and went inside. After they shut and locked the door, they heard the car and truck start up and pull away.

"Are you hungry?" asked Maddie.

June thought for a minute.

"Yes, I am. I had not thought it until now, but I would like a snack," she said.

"Me, too," said Maddie. "Let's see what Dora has in the refrigerator."

The girls headed for the kitchen.

Maddie found some tomatoes and some chicken salad. She cut the tomatoes and added some chicken salad to the plate. She put the two plates on the bar and got two glasses of tea. June pulled out two forks and the girls sat on the bar stools to enjoy their midnight feast.

"Ummm, this is so good," said June.

"Yes," agreed Maddie.

The girls finished their food and cleaned up after themselves.

They were just about to go upstairs when both of their phones rang. They hurried to answer them before they woke anyone.

"Hello, Liam," said Maddie.

At the same time, June answered Jason.

"I just wanted to say, I love you," said Liam.

"I love you, too," said Maddie.

"Dream of me," said Liam.

"I have been dreaming of you for four years. I intend to do much more than dream now," said Maddie.

Liam laughed. "I can't wait. Good night, Love."

They hung up and Maddie waved at June, who was still talking to Jason, and went upstairs. June soon was following her upstairs to bed. Both young ladies were very happy with their lives.

CHAPTER 8

*D*ora and Rafe were getting ready to leave for church the next morning when Maddie and June joined them in the kitchen.

"Good morning," said Dora. "The coffee is made and there are blueberry muffins in a basket on the table. We have to go in early. I'm teaching Dede's Sunday school class. Her regular teacher is on bed rest because of a difficult pregnancy."

"I know how much you enjoy teaching Sunday school," said Maddie, getting two cups and pouring her and June coffee.

"Yes, I do, but I hope her teacher is doing okay," said Dora.

"Come on, Dede, were ready to go," called Rafe as he came down the stairs. "Good morning, Maddie and June." He came over and kissed each on the cheek before continuing on out the door to get the car.

Dede hurried in and came to give Maddie a hug. She looked at June as if she did not quite know how to greet her.

June smiled at her and said good morning.

Dede smiled back and relaxed. Dora told them to help themselves and ushered Dede out the door to where Rafe was waiting with the car already running.

Maddie smiled at June as they sat down to enjoy their coffee and muffins.

"Dede is still a little shy around you," she told June. "She will warm up fast when she gets to know you a little better."

June smiled. "I know, we have all the time we need," she replied.

"Yes," agreed Maddie happily.

They finished their coffee and ate their muffins and were cleaning up after themselves when they heard the car and truck pull up into the driveway.

Maddie grinned and took down two napkins. She wrapped a muffin in each and gave one to June. June grinned and took the muffin. The girls headed for the front door.

Maddie opened the door and Liam pulled her into a hug. While they were kissing, Jason went around them and pulled June into a similar hug. Both Maddie and June were holding a hand out so the muffins did not get smashed.

When Liam loosened up his hold, he glanced at Maddie's outstretched arm. He grinned and sniffed.

"Is that what I think it is?" he asked.

"If you think it is a blueberry muffin, it is," said Maddie with a grin.

Liam kissed her again.

"Thank you," he said. He took the muffin and ate it on the way to the car.

Meanwhile, Jason had managed to eat his muffin while holding onto June and getting her into his truck.

They drove to the church and parked next to each other. The guys held onto their girls as they led the way into the church and down to the aisle where their mom and sisters were sitting. Jason went into the aisle first, holding onto June's hand so she was following him. Maddie followed June and Liam came last. They all greeted Madeline, Meg and Anna, and were greeted in return.

Maddie spotted Blake in an aisle across from them. He was seated with his housekeeper, Mrs. Shell. Maddie smiled and waved at Blake and Mrs. Shell.

Mrs. Shell had been Blake's housekeeper for about a year and a half. They got along very well, and Blake was happy to have her working for him. She had been a former client of his. She was looking for a place to move to and Blake offered her a position in his home. It had been a happy solution for both of them.

She moved into the rooms off the kitchen. They had been occupied at one time by Aunt Mary, and then Ruby and Harry used them for a while. It gave Mrs. Shell some privacy and gave Blake the peace of mind knowing his house was occupied when he wasn't there. He also liked having her there to cook for him, except on Saturday, her day off. She spent her Saturdays with her grandchildren, and Blake usually ate out.

Dora, Dede and Rafe joined them and sat in the seats in front of them. They all turned and smiled. The preacher came in and stood at the podium.

"We have a treat for you this morning. I asked Dora to sing and she said she would if her sister would join her. So, how about it, Maddie?" He looked at Maddie and waited. Dora had already risen and was waiting for Maddie. Maddie rose and waited for Liam to rise and let her out. He squeezed her hand in encouragement as she passed him.

"I thought we could sing the old rugged cross," said Dora.

Maddie nodded her agreement and Dora went over to the organ to tell the lady who would play their selection.

Dora and Maddie had sung together many times in

church. They did not need the book to sing. Both girls stood straight and solemn. They looked at the cross at the back of the chapel and sang in perfect harmony with each other.

It was very quiet for a minute after they finished the song, and then applause started. Everyone stood and applauded. Maddie and Dora bowed slightly and then headed for their seats. As Liam got out, letting Maddie in, he smiled and kissed her on the nose. Maddie grinned at him and took her seat.

Dora took her seat next to Rafe. He put his arm around her and pulled her close. She looked up at him and grinned. He leaned forward and kissed the tip of her nose and gave her another squeeze. Dora sighed. She was so happy the mirror had shown her true love to her. This family was her heart. They completed her.

The preacher thanked them for singing and launched into his sermon.

After the service was over and everyone rose for the final song, Maddie glanced back and saw Lars seated with some of his friends. She smiled at him, and he smiled back. They both began to sing the final song selection.

After church, they caught up with Blake and Mrs. Shell. They greeted each other and stood to one side out of the way of others leaving. They did not get any time for private conversation. There were too many people around. Blake asked Dora if all of them would like to come to his house for a meal. Dora declined.

"I have dinner cooking in the crock pot and a ham that I baked yesterday. Why don't you and Mrs. Shell join us?" she asked.

Blake looked at Mrs. Shell inquiringly. She nodded okay, so Blake smiled and accepted.

"I want to go home first and change into something more comfortable.

We will be on in a little while," agreed Blake.

They all piled into their vehicles and headed for home. Madeline and the girls were joining them also, and Madeline was bringing dessert.

When they arrived at Rafe and Doras', everyone went to their rooms to change out of their church clothes. Jason and Liam left to go home and change. They were back by the time everyone was downstairs.

"Rafe, you take Jason, Liam and Lars outside to shoot hoops or something while we get dinner on the table," said Dora.

"Okay, you just want us out of your way," replied Rafe with a kiss.

"Yes," agreed Dora with a smile. "Now, scoot."

"We are going," said Jason throwing his hands up in surrender.

He gave June a quick kiss and followed Rafe out of the front door. Liam gave Maddie a kiss and followed his brothers. He grabbed Lars' arm and took him along with him.

Dora smiled at Maddie and June.

"Dede is in her room. She will be down soon. Let's get to the kitchen before those guys think up an excuse to come back in," said Dora. "Otherwise, they will eat everything, and we won't have anything left for lunch." Maddie and June laughed and followed her.

"If you get some bowls and set them on the counter, we can fill them up and let each person take their own bowl to the table," she said.

Maddie took the bowls out of the cabinet and put them on the counter next to the crock pot.

"Do you want plates on the table?" asked June.

"Yes, they are in the cabinet," said Dora, pointing at a cabinet.

"Maddie, could you help me place this ham in the center of the table?" asked Dora.

"Sure," said Maddie hurrying to help. They lifted the ham out of the oven and settled it in the center of the table.

"Now, we need to put napkins in those two baskets and fill them with the garlic rolls I have warming in the warming oven," said Dora. She stood back and surveyed her table. "Now all we need are utensils and glasses for the tea," she said.

"I'll get the utensils," said June.

"I'll get the glasses," said Maddie.

"Ready for dessert?" asked Madeline as she Anna and Meg entered.

'Yes, we are," smiled Dora. "Let's put it over on the counter. If it is on the table, the guys will eat it first."

She took one of the pie containers from Meg and carried it to the counter.

"Oh, it smells so good. Apple?" she asked.

"Yes, I have two apple pies and a peach cobbler," said Madeline.

"Ummm, I just might skip straight to dessert, myself," said Dora.

"Anna, would you ask Dede to join us? You may have to go upstairs. She probably has her earphones on," said Dora.

Mrs. Shell entered the kitchen. She had a large bowl of salad. "Blake joined the guys out front. He told me to come on in," she said. Maddie hurried to take the salad and put it in the center of the table with the ham.

Dora came over and gave Mrs. Shell a hug. "We are glad you could join us. The salad looks so good. I'm going to have to watch my food intake. Since I became pregnant, I am craving everything," said Dora. The other ladies laughed.

Dede and Anna came in and Dede looked at all of the food. "I would have helped if you had called me," she said.

Dora came over and gave her a hug. "I know sweetie. I just wanted to spend a little time with my sister. You can help clean up," said Dora.

"Okay," agreed Dede.

"Maddie would you and June call the guys to the table while I get out the knife and ladle?" asked Dora.

"Sure," said Maddie as she and June headed for the front door.

They stepped out on the porch and stood watching as the guys ran around shooting hoops.

Jason glanced over and saw June. Rafe ran by him and took the ball. Jason just grinned and headed for June. As soon as he was close enough, he put his arm around her and hugged her to his side. Liam, seeing Maddie, abandoned the game and headed for her. Blake looked over and grinned.

"It looks like the game is over. Lunch must be ready," he said.

Rafe grinned and slung an arm around Lars' neck and headed for the porch. "Break it up," said Rafe to Jason and Liam. "Let's eat." They all entered and headed for the dining room.

"Stop right there," said Dora holding up a hand. "Hand washing first," The guys turned and headed for the bathroom to wash their hands.

They were just about to sit down, when the Judge and Lucy suddenly appeared. "Mom, Dad," exclaimed Dora as she Maddie and Blake hurried to greet their parents.

"We decided to see for ourselves how you all were doing," said Lucy.

"Mom you don't need an excuse to visit. You and Dad are welcome anytime," said Dora.

Dede and Lars came over and gave their grandparents hugs.

While everyone was busy with greetings, June laid out two more place settings and put out more bowls and glasses. Dora, seeing what she was doing, gave her a hug and said a quiet thank you. June just smiled at her.

"Let's all sit and eat. There are bowls on the counter for the stew," said Dora. She handed Rafe the knife so he could cut the ham.

Everyone lined up and filled their bowls. When they were through, they all sat down and joining hands, the Judge led them in the blessing.

They all dug in. The salad bowl was passed around and was soon empty. Rafe passed out ham to any who asked and the garlic bread disappeared quickly. When they were finished with all of the food, Dora looked around and smiled.

"Who is ready for dessert?" she asked.

There were several groans, but when she and Maddie and Meg brought the apple pies and peach cobbler to the table, they all perked up. No one turned down dessert. The dessert plates were soon clean.

Maddie and Dede started stacking the dishes to clean the table, but Jason, Rafe, Liam and Blake shooed them out with instructions to rest and visit. They would clean up.

The girls left them to it and went out on the porch where everyone was sitting.

The Judge and Lucy were sitting in one of the swings with Lars in between them. The Judge was very fond of Lars. When Dora and Rafe were married and Dora adopted both Dede and Lars, the Judge accepted them as his grandchildren and set up trust funds for each of them. He said he just wanted them to be able to have options in life.

Dora was sitting in the other swing with Mrs. Shell.

Madeline had taken a rocker to sit in close to Lucy, so they could talk. Anna and Meg were sitting on the porch leaning back against the rail. Maddie and June sat down on the steps, one on each side with a wide space in between.

When the guys came out, Rafe took Dora's hand and led her to a rocker and sat down with her in his lap. Blake took the seat vacated by Dora, and Liam and Jason sat on the steps with Maddie and June.

Maddie smiled at Liam as he slid in behind her and leaned against the post so she could lean against him. Jason did the same with June.

The Judge looked around and smiled. He was happy to see his family so happy and content. Even though Blake had not found a life partner, yet, he looked happy.

"How is Maddie and June's school coming along," the Judge asked Blake.

"Everything is in order. The bid has been accepted and Maddie and June can sign the papers tomorrow. It will take about a week to finalize everything, but they can start making plans as soon as the papers are signed.

Maddie squealed and jumping up ran over and hugged Blake. She then grabbed June's hands and pulled her up and started dancing around the porch with her.

"We are going to have our school," she said. Everyone laughed at her excitement.

Maddie went over and hugged her parents. "Thank you, so much for helping my dream come true," she said.

"We will always be here for you. Do not ever forget you have parents who love you very much," said Lucy.

"Yes," agreed the Judge. He looked sternly at Jason and Liam. "You guys had better take very good care of my girls."

"Yes, Sir, we will," said Liam. "I love your daughter very much. Her happiness will always be my top priority."

"June is my life," said Jason. "I will do anything to make her happy."

The Judge smiled at them and then at Lucy.

"Doesn't that remind you of when I had to face your father and tell him we were getting married?" he asked Lucy.

"Yes," agreed Lucy. "We were both shaking in our shoes."

"Well," said the Judge. "We had better get started for home. We have a long drive ahead of us."

They got up and started hugging everyone goodbye. Blake and Mrs. Shell started their goodbyes, also. Maddie ran inside and brought back Mrs. Shell's large salad bowl. After they were gone, they rearranged the seating on the porch. Liam and Maddie took one swing and Jason and June took the other. Maddie made room for Lars to sit with her and Liam, and June and Jason made room for Dede.

The guys did not care who else was there so long as they could hold their ladies in their arms. It was a pleasant time for all.

CHAPTER 9

*J*ason and Liam had to work the next day, so Maddie and June headed in to see Blake and sign the papers for their new martial arts school. When they entered Blake's office, the receptionist told them Blake was expecting them and to go on in.

Maddie knocked on Blake's door and entered when he said 'come in'.

Blake looked up from his desk and smiled at them. "Hello. Where are your shadows?" he asked.

"Jason and Liam had to work at the logging site," said Maddie, smiling back at him. "We wanted to get the papers signed for our school and gym."

"I have everything ready," said Blake, opening a folder. "Have a seat and you can look over the papers."

Maddie and June sat in the chairs in front of Blake's desk and each took some of the papers to look over. When each finished her papers, she switched and looked over the others. Maddie finished her papers and looked at Blake.

"It looks very straight forward to me. Of course, I know

you will look out for me. What about the operating permits we will need?" she asked.

"They won't be a problem. Rafe is head of the Chamber of Commerce. I have already sent him the papers needed to get your permits. He will look them over and send them to the proper departments. You should have them by the time the purchase is finalized."

"Great," said Maddie. "It helps to have family around."

"Yes, it does, sometimes," agreed June.

"That reminds me, June, I met your sister, Saturday," said Blake. "I thought it was you at first. I went over to say hello and she told me she wasn't you."

"You met July?" asked June startled.

"Yes, at the seafood restaurant," said Blake.

"I did not know she was in town," said June.

"She said she was starting work at Dulcie's hair salon today," said Blake.

"I wonder why she picked here," said June.

"Maybe she just wanted to be close to you," said Blake.

"I don't think so," said June shaking her head.

She looked over at Maddie and found Maddie looking back thoughtfully. "Are you sure she did not know about you seeing Jason in the mirror?" asked Maddie.

"I don't see how. I did not say anything about it to anyone. Besides, I did not know who he was, then. I sure did not know where he lived," responded June.

"Jason and his crew delivered some logs in Denton not long ago. Maybe she saw him then," said Maddie.

"Yes, the first time I talked to Jason in the mirror, he mentioned he had met July in Denton," agreed June.

Blake followed this conversation before saying anything. "I take it, you and your sister are not close," he said.

June shrugged her shoulder. "Not really, July steered clear of me for the last couple of years. She did not want to help me take care of Mom while she was sick. Maybe she has lightened up since Mom remarried and moved to Australia," said June.

June did not want to get into her family history with Blake. She did not know him very well.

Maddie could see June did not want to talk about July, so she started signing papers and passing them on to June for her to sign.

When they had finished, Maddie sat back with a smile of satisfaction.

Blake took the papers and checked to make sure everything was signed and then handed Maddie a ring of keys.

"It will be yours in a week, but I thought you might start looking around and planning what renovations will be needed. I already checked with the sellers. They have no objections. So have fun," Blake smiled and ushered the girls out with a hug for each.

The girls piled into Maddie's car and drove up the block to their new school. Maddie parked in front and they got out. Maddie got goose bumps, using the key for the first time. They went in, and June pulled out a tablet and a pen and started making notes while they walked around.

They finished the front building with a lot of notes to go over later. Then, they came to the door to the back room. It was going to be converted to a gym, and they really did not know what all would be needed. They would have to get some expert advice on it.

Maddie unlocked the door, and they eased into the room. Maddie had a weird feeling, but she did not know why. It was just another building.

They heard a rustling sound over in the corner.

"Maybe we have mice," said June.

"Maybe," said Maddie, heading to the corner to check it out.

There were some large boxes there and she shifted them around so she could see.

"Oh, my goodness!" she exclaimed.

"What is it?" asked June.

"Look what I found," said Maddie.

June hurried over and knelt beside Maddie, who was kneeling beside a baby and a small girl. The baby was squirming and the little girl was looking at Maddie and June. She looked very scared and clutched the baby closer to her.

"It's alright," Maddie said soothingly. "We won't hurt you."

She reached over and rubbed the child gently on top of her head.

The girl seemed to shrink away from her.

"What's your name, Sweetie?" asked June.

"My name is Cathy Savolt. This is my brother Max. Momma left us here yesterday and told us to stay until she comes back for us, but Max has used up his milk bottles and he is hungry," the little girl had tears running down her face.

June drew her into her arms and soothed her.

Maddie picked up the baby, and he quieted momentarily. Maddie took her phone and called Chief Stan Welldon.

"Hello, Chief Welldon's office," said a voice.

"Hello, this is Maddie Hawthorn. May I speak with Chief Welldon?"

"Hello, Miss Hawthorn. How are you?" asked Chief Welldon.

"I'm not doing so good right now. I have a situation at my

new karate school. Could you come over? I'm in the back room," said Maddie.

"I'll be right there," said the Chief.

"You going out, Chief?" asked the Desk Clerk.

"Yes, I'll be at the new karate school. Maddie Hawthorn called and said she had a situation there," he said.

"What kind of situation?" asked the Clerk.

"I don't know, but I have learned not to ignore the Hawthorns," he said as he went out the door.

"Hello," called the Chief from the front room.

"We are back here," called Maddie.

The Chief went into the back room and stopped short when he saw Maddie and June sitting on the floor cradling the two children. Maddie got up, still holding the baby and went over to speak to the Chief.

"We found these two when we were looking around. The little girl said she is five and her name is Cathy Savolt. Her brother is one and his name is Max. She said her mother put them in here yesterday and told them to stay until she came back for them," said Maddie.

"I don't think she will be back," said the Chief, thoughtfully.

"Why not?" asked Maddie.

"Their mother and father were pushed off the road in their car. They were a few miles out of town. Their car crashed and burned. Everyone assumed their children were in the car with them. If we turn these children over to CPS, they could become targets of whoever killed their parents."

He and Maddie were quiet for a few minutes thinking.

"Chief, do you think you could get me a couple of car seats for my car?" asked Maddie, "Get one for a five-year-old and one for an infant. Do it quietly so no one will talk.".

"Yes, I can do that," he said. "What are you going to do?"

"Chief I want you to meet my niece and nephew. They are my sister's children. This is Adam and the little girl is Sissy. They are going to be staying with me for a while," said Maddie.

The Chief started grinning. Maddie smiled back at him.

"I'll go get those seats," he said.

When he was gone, she went over to June. June had heard most of the conversation, but she had tried to keep Cathy occupied.

Maddie sat down next to June and Cathy.

"Cathy, we are going to play a game. From now on, if anyone asks your name, just tell them you are Sissy and this is your brother Adam. You can call me Aunt Maddie and call June, Aunt June. Do you think you can remember all of that?" asked Maddie.

Cathy nodded her head sleepily and leaned her head against June and closed her eyes.

"I have the seats, and I installed them in your car," said the Chief from the door.

"While we put the children in the car, Chief, could you gather up all of their stuff so there will be no sign they were ever here?" asked Maddie.

The Chief went to clean up while the girls put the children in the car.

When they had the children secured in the car, Maddie saw the Chief come out of the front door. She left June and the children and went to lock the front door.

"Thanks, Chief Welldon. Let me know if you hear anything," said Maddie.

"Thank you, Miss Maddie. I will keep in touch. Let me know if you find anything suspicious. I do not want to put your family in danger," said the Chief.

"I'll call you if there are any problems," promised Maddie.

With a wave she returned to the car and headed for Madeline's.

"Why are we going to Madeline's instead of Dora's?" asked June.

"Because Dora is pregnant and I do not want to cause her any stress. Madeline has more experience with babies. She also has Meg and Anna to help out. We can help out until our school is up and running," said Maddie.

"I am going to call Blake and get him to stop by after work. I do not want to discuss the situation on the phone. With technology these days you never know who is listening to your conversation," said Maddie.

"I know what you mean," agreed June.

"I'll call Rafe and find out where Jason and Liam are. We can see when they will be home and talk to them then," said Maddie as she piled into Madeline's front driveway.

They got out and Maddie took the baby, while June unstrapped the little girl. She was sound asleep. They carried the children up the porch steps and across the porch. Madeline opened the door before they could knock.

"What have we here?" she asked.

"We need your help," said Maddie.

"We found these two children in the back room of our school. They were hidden under a large box," said June.

"Did you report it?" asked Madeline.

"Yes, I did," said Maddie. "I called the Chief. He said everyone thinks they are dead. Someone deliberately caused their parents' car to crash and burn. He doesn't want anyone to know they are alive. He's afraid they will come after the children."

"Poor kids," said Madeline.

"I told him to tell anyone interested that they are my

sister's children, Sissy and Adam. I am taking care of them for a while."

Meg and Anna had come in and listened to everything.

"I know they are hungry. They had been in the back room overnight and the baby had run out of milk," said June.

Meg took the baby and headed for the kitchen to feed him. The others followed her with Cathy, still sleeping.

"Poor thing is probably exhausted. She was too scared to get much sleep last night. She had to look after her brother, too," said Maddie.

While Madeline made some soup, Cathy woke up. "What's that smell?"

June poured some soup into a bowl and brought it over to Cathy, for her to eat. Maddie took her phone out and called Blake.

"Hello," said Blake.

"Hi, we looked around and made some lists," said Maddie. "Do you think you could stop by Madeline's after work? I want to discuss something with you," said Maddie.

"Sure," said Blake. "Do you need me to come now?"

"No, after work will be fine," said Maddie.

"Alright, I will see you, then," Blake hung up the phone and frowned. Maddie sounded strange. Not at all like herself.

Maddie then called Rafe.

"Hello, Maddie," said Rafe.

"Hi, Rafe, are Liam or Jason around?"

"No, they are out at Jason's house. The crew is working there today. Why?" he asked.

"When they get off, could all of you stop by your mother's house? I want to talk to you all about something.

"Sure, you want me to bring Dora, too?" he asked.

"Yes, please," said Maddie.

"Alright, we will see you, then. You are alright, aren't you?" he asked.

"I'm fine. I'll see you when you get here."

Maddie hung up the phone with a sigh and headed for the kitchen.

CHAPTER 10

*T*hey were all sitting in the front room, quietly talking. June was sitting on the love seat. Cathy had her head in June's lap and was covered with a blanket. She had clung to June and would not settle to sleep anywhere else. Meg and Anna brought down a play pen and set it up for the baby. They both were bathed and fed. They were sleeping soundly. Maddie was seated in one of the rockers and Madeline was in another. Meg and Anna were seated on a bench under the front window. They had been talking quietly, so they would not disturb the children.

The door burst open, admitting Jason, Liam, Rafe, Dora. Dede, Lars, and, Blake. They started to speak, but were quieted with a Shhhhh from Madeline, Maddie, June, Anna, and Meg. They all stopped and looked around. Jason made his way over to June and leaned over and kissed her. He rubbed a hand gently over Cathy's head.

"Daddy," murmured Cathy and clutched his finger.

Jason smiled and tried to loosen his hand, but Cathy just clutched it tighter. Jason smiled at June and sat down on the floor and leaned against her leg so as not to disturb the sleeping little girl. June smiled at Jason and, leaning forward, kissed him on the top of his head. Maddie was right, she thought. Jason was a big softie.

Liam went over to Maddie and pulled her up and sitting down, seated her in his lap.

"What's going on?" he asked quietly.

Rafe and Dora sat on the sofa. Dede sat with them. Blake and Lars had found chairs to sit in. Everyone was waiting for an explanation.

"June and I found these two in the back room of our new school this morning," said Maddie.

"Did you call the Chief?" asked Blake.

Maddie frowned at Blake. "Yes, I did." said Maddie. "It seems these two are orphans. Someone ran their parents off the road a few miles out of town. Their car crashed and burned. Everyone thinks the children were in the car with them, but their mother had hidden them in our back room and told them she would be back for them. The Chief was afraid if anyone knew they were still alive, they would come after them. I told him we would take care of them for now. If anyone asks, they are Rena's kids, Sissy and Adam. We are just taking care of them for her for a while."

Maddie stopped talking and looked around expectantly. Everyone was quiet thinking about what they had just heard.

"You could have brought them to our house," said Dora.

Maddie was shaking her head. "Madeline was the best choice," she said. "You and Rafe have to work. Madeline and the girls are here all day, and June and I can help until we get our school up and running. I asked all of you here, because I did not want to discuss this on the phone. Sometimes phones can be listened in on. You cannot tell anyone about this. Not even your best friends," she said.

She looked at Dede and Lars, who both nodded their understanding.

"These children's lives could depend on no one knowing they survived," she said.

Blake looked at Maddie and shook his head. "What is it?" asked Maddie.

"I have some amazing sisters," he replied.

"Yes, you do," agreed Liam and Jason, and Rafe.

"So, what happens now?" asked Lars.

"We have already talked to Madeline about this," said Maddie. "June and I are going to stay here until we see what's going to happen. Cathy will not let June out of her sight and she gets fretful if she does not know where her brother is. We can share a room, and if they wake up at night, we will be able to quieten them."

Liam smiled. He was all for Maddie being closer.

Jason was thinking the same thing. He squeezed June's knee with his free hand. He looked at the tiny girl who was clutching his finger so tightly. He smiled and felt his heart quicken. Such a beautiful child. So much sorrow to go through for one so young. It reminded him of Dede and Lars when his brother died. He looked at June, and she smiled at him in perfect understanding. He squeezed her knee again.

"If you need any help with anything, you come to us," said Rafe.

"If you get suspicious of anyone, you let us know immediately," said Blake.

"We will. I have already promised the Chief to keep him informed," said Maddie.

"You will have Jason and Liam here with you at night, but I don't like the idea of you ladies being alone all day while everyone is working," said Blake.

"We will be fine," said Maddie. "June and I are both black

belts and Madeline and I put two shotguns in the closet by the front door and one by the back door."

"It sounds like you are prepared for war," said Lars.

"If anyone tries to hurt these children, they will be wishing they only had to contend with a war," said June. Everyone smiled at this comment.

Blake was the first to stand and get ready to leave. Rafe and Dora followed after him. Dede went with them, but Lars asked to stay the night. Madeline quickly agreed before His parents could veto the idea. Rafe just smiled and shook his head. Dora hugged him and told him to behave.

When everyone who was leaving had left, Madeline and Meg headed for the kitchen to fix something to eat.

Maddie stirred, and turning in his arms, kissed Liam.

"I should go help your mom in the kitchen," she said.

"Not yet," said Liam. "I missed you today."

"I missed you, too," agreed Maddie returning his kiss.

There was a knock at the front door. Lars headed for the door to open it. Maddie held up a hand to stop him.

"Ask who it is before you open the door," she said.

"Who is it?" called Lars obediently.

"Chief Welldon," was the reply.

Lars opened the door. The Chief reached over and ruffled his hair.

"Good job," he replied.

"Aunt Maddie told me to ask," said Lars.

"Is there any news, Chief?" asked Maddie.

"I received pictures of the children's parents. I thought you might want to take a look at them," he said. He handed the pictures to Maddie and Liam.

"Oh my!" exclaimed Maddie.

"What is it?" asked Madeline. She had heard someone come in and came to see who it was.

"It is a picture of the children's parents. The father looks just like Jason," said Liam.

"Let me see it," said Madeline. She looked at the picture in amazement. "What was the parent's name?" she asked.

"The father's name was Anthony Savolt. His wife's name was Liz," said the Chief.

Lars had taken the picture over to Jason and June. They looked at it in amazement.

"Amos, my husband, had an older sister named Amelia. She married a Savolt. She did not stay in touch with us afterwards. Amos did not like the guy at all. He tried to talk her out of marrying him, but she ran away with him and married him anyway. I guess this Anthony Savolt must have been her son. The children are your cousins," she told everyone.

"No wonder she thought Jason was her Daddy," said June.

"Well, I haven't heard anything else. I guess Mr. Savolt must have tangled with the wrong people," said the Chief.

"As long as they do not come after the children, we will leave all of Mr. Savolt's problems in your hands, Chief. I hope these people do not know about the connection to our family," said Jason.

"Keep them out of town and watch out. Maybe whoever is responsible for their deaths will move on or trip up so we can catch them," said the Chief.

"If you need any help, just call us," said Jason grinning. "You can always deputize us to help."

June hit him on his shoulder.

"Oh," he said startled.

"You are not going out after some murderers. We are not married, yet. I intend to be married for a very long time. You let the Chief handle the law," she said.

"Yes, Ma'am," agreed Jason with a grin. June leaned forward and gave him a kiss.

Everyone smiled at their antics. It lightened the atmosphere considerably.

"I had better get back to town. I just couldn't believe it when I saw the picture. I put the rest of them in my car. I did not want word to spread about him being a Jason look alike," said the Chief. "Good night, everyone."

Everyone called out good night and Madeline headed back to the kitchen.

"Well, I guess it is true. Everyone does have a look alike," said Jason.

"Oh, I forgot to tell you. According to Blake, my sister July is in town. She supposedly is taking a job at Dulcie's hair salon," said June.

Jason frowned. "I hope she is not planning to cause any trouble," he remarked.

"Don't worry, I can handle her. As long as I know you love me, July is not important," said June.

She leaned forward for another kiss. Cathy stirred and let go of Jason's finger. June eased out from under her and slid down onto the floor into Jason's arms.

CHAPTER 11

*T*he next morning, both Liam and Jason were reluctant to leave. They hated the idea of their family being in danger. Madeline shooed them out after breakfast. She assured them everything would be alright. No one knew of the connection between them and the children's parents.

"We have our phones. You are just going to be working on Jason's house. I'll fix lunch. You can check in then. Now, go on and get to work. Tell Rafe about our connection to the children. He and Dora had left last night before we found out about it," Madeline instructed.

They left reluctantly, after taking Maddie and June onto the porch for a final kiss.

"You'll call if you need us? We can be here in minutes," said Liam.

"Yes," said Maddie.

"Promise," said Jason.

"Promise," said June

They left and the girls waved goodbye. They went inside to check on the children.

After breakfast, they put the baby down for a nap. He still seemed very tired. They put him in the play pen in the front room and turned on a cartoon for Cathy to watch. Anna stayed in the room with them and quietly kept watch over them.

June, Maddie, and Meg helped Madeline straighten the house. They made beds and gathered dirty clothes and took them to the laundry room. They sorted the clothes and put in a load to wash. Madeline put a roast in to cook for lunch along with some vegetables in the crock pot. She made several loaves of bread and put them back to rise, so they could be baked later.

June and Maddie finished their chores and went out on the porch to relax and swing for a while. They had checked on the children, and they were doing okay.

They had only been relaxing a short while when Chief Welldon drove up. He got out of his car and joined the girls on the porch. They both watched him warily, hoping he did not have any more bad news.

"Morning," he said.

"Good morning,' they both replied.

"Has there been any news?" asked Maddie.

"Yes," replied the Chief. "It looks like the children are in the clear. I got a bulletin from the state police. They caught the ones responsible for the Savolt's death. There was a shoot-out and both men are dead."

"Did they find out why they did it?" asked June.

"It turns out one of the men, Sam Simon, was Liz's ex-husband. He had been in prison for eight years for armed robbery of a gas one-stop store. He was sent up for twenty-five years and Liz was granted a divorce. She married Savolt two years later. Simon and another prisoner escaped about a week ago."

"Anthony and Liz were probably headed here to ask the family for help," said Maddie.

"That is my guess," said the Chief. "She must have felt Simon closing in and hidden the children."

"Did either of them have any relatives," asked June.

"Liz was an orphan. Anthony has a mother in a nursing home. I think the state police were going to get in touch with her," he said.

"Can you call them back and stop them. Jason will want to go and see her and see if he can help her. She should not have to receive such news from the police. I know she doesn't know the family, but we all want to be there for her," said June.

"Yes," agreed Maddie. "We also have to ask her about the children."

"Alright," said Chief Welldon. "I'll see if I can stop them. I will hold back on any reports about the children until you talk to her."

The Chief said goodbye and left.

June took out her phone to call Jason and Maddie called Liam.

They both told the guys what the Chief had just told them.

"Alright," said Jason. "Liam can go and tell Rafe what is going on and I will give the guys here instructions on what to do next. We will both be home in about a half hour."

"Okay, I love you," said June.

"I love you, too," said Jason.

They both hung up. Maddie and June went inside to tell Madeline what was going on. They told Madeline and Meg the news in the kitchen and then went into the front room and sat down with the children. The baby was awake and Anna was feeding him his bottle while Cathy looked on. June sat down in the floor and pulled Cathy into her lap. Maddie took the baby from Anna and resumed his feeding. She sat on the love seat.

"When are my mommy and daddy coming?" asked Cathy.

June hugged her and held her close.

"Your mommy and daddy have gone to heaven to look after your granddad. They are not going to be back," said June.

"Who's going to look after me and Max?" asked Cathy tearfully.

"Well your mommy and daddy left you here for me and Jason to look after. Would it be alright with you if we look after you and Max?" she asked.

Cathy looked at her searchingly. She seemed to be satisfied with what she saw, because she nodded her head and snuggled closer to June.

Jason had come in the door when June started talking to Cathy. He stood and listened. He started smiling. He had picked a winner. He was so very proud of her. Madeline was also listening. She smiled at Jason through her tears. She had a great family, and it just kept getting better.

Liam followed Jason in, and Rafe came in shortly after. He had called Dora and filled her in on the way home. She was getting someone to take her class and then she would be here.

"I need to call Blake," said Maddie. "He will want to know what is going on."

Jason sat on the floor and put an arm around June and Cathy. He kissed June, and then he kissed Cathy on top of her head.

"I love you," he said.

"I love you, too," said June.

Cathy was watching Jason and June closely.

"You look like my daddy. Are you going to be my new daddy?" she asked.

"I would love to be your new daddy," said Jason.

"Baby Max, too?" she asked.

"Baby Max, too," agreed Jason.

Cathy settled back against June, satisfied.

Liam went over and sat beside Maddie. Maddie handed him Max and the bottle, so he could feed him while Maddie called Blake.

Maddie decided to go out on the porch while she talked to Blake, so the children would not hear. Jason came out when she finished explaining things and asked to speak to Blake.

"Hello, Blake, do you think you could go with us to break the news to Amelia about her son and his wife's death? I want to take some papers for her to sign, giving June and me the right to adopt the children. She is in a nursing home. I don't think she is in any position to care for them.

"Yes, I can go," said Blake. "Do you know where the nursing home is?"

"No, could you call the Chief and get an address for it?"

"Okay," agreed Blake."

"Rafe is going with us, so we will see you in about an hour," said Jason.

Jason went back inside to tell Rafe and June his plan.

Rafe heard Dora's car pull up, so he went out on the porch to fill her in and let her know he was going with Jason and Blake to see Amelia.

Dora hugged him close and told him to be careful. Rafe hugged her back and kissed her.

"Don't worry. I'll be back as soon as I can. I love you," he said.

Dora kissed him and hugged him close again. They then went inside to greet everyone.

Dora smiled to see Jason seated on the floor with June, with his arms around June and Cathy.

"We have to go," said Jason getting up and helping June and Cathy up. "I told Blake we would meet him in an hour." Rafe and Jason said goodbye and headed for Rafe's car. Everyone stood on the porch and waved goodbye.

Blake was waiting out in front of his office holding his briefcase.

Rafe pulled up next to him and stopped. Blake entered the back seat and fastened his seatbelt. "Did you get the address?" asked Rafe.

"Yes, she is in Garden Springs Nursing Home. It is about an hour northwest of here, said Blake.

"I know where Garden Springs is," said Jason. "We have made log deliveries there."

Rafe made his way to the highway and headed toward Garden Springs.

"Did you get the papers for her to sign, consenting to the adoption?" asked Jason.

"Yes, I have the papers. When she signs them, you will still have to go before a judge and get him to sign off on them," said Blake.

"I know," replied Jason. "We went through all of that when Rafe adopted Dede and Lars. I don't think we will have any problem getting a judge to sign the papers."

Rafe looked over and grinned at his brother. He was so glad Jason was finally getting the life he had been searching for.

"Have you seen any more of June's sister July?" Jason asked Blake.

"No, I have been pretty busy. She is probably busy getting

started in her new job," answered Blake. "What is it with her and June? Do they not get along?"

"I don't know the whole story. I just know June is wary of July. She seems to want to avoid her. I think part of their problems began when their mother was sick and July refused to be around her. She left all of her care to June and June had to drop out of the university to take care of her," remarked Jason.

"Well, I hope they can get past the hard feelings now. With their mother in Australia, they only have each other here in the states," remarked Blake.

"June has me and soon Cathy and Max will be our family. If July wants to be a part of our family, she will have to work it out with June. I will stand by whatever June decides," Jason declared.

Blake nodded his head and dropped the subject. Rafe had been quietly listening to the new note of maturity in Jason's voice. He smiled. He was happy for his brother.

They were quiet as they sped down the highway towards Garden Springs.

It was about 2 o'clock when they stopped in front of the Garden Springs Nursing Home and exited the car before going inside.

They went up to the front desk.

"Excuse me," said Rafe. "We would like to see our Aunt, Amelia Savolt."

The nurse looked down at her computer screen.

"You are not listed on her visitor's list," she said.

"Her son and his wife were killed in a car accident. We need to break the news and get her permission to take care of her grandchildren," said Rafe. Jason and Blake were quietly standing behind Rafe, letting him handle things.

The nurse looked visibly shaken. She came from behind

the desk and motioned for them to follow her. She tapped softly on a door and entered at a "Come in."

"Mrs. Savolt, you have visitors," she said. She entered the room and Rafe, Jason and Blake followed her in.

Amelia stared at the men entering her room. She knew they had to be Amos' boys because one of them looked so much like Anthony. She shivered as a feeling of dread washed over her.

Rafe went over to her bedside and took her hand. "Aunt Amelia, I am Rafe. This is my brother Jason and my wife's brother Blake. We are so sorry we did not get to know you before now."

Amelia looked up at him tearfully. "Anthony is gone," she said.

Rafe nodded. He and his wife Liz were killed in a car crash," he confirmed.

"Amelia smothered a cry. "What about the children?"

"We have the children at our place. They are fine," said Jason.

"What is going to happen to them?" asked Amelia.

"If it is alright with you, my wife June and I would like to adopt them. We have to do it quickly before they get put in the system. It will be hard to get them out once they are entered," said Jason.

Amelia gave Jason a long searching look and then she smiled. "I will be happy for you to take my grandchildren," she said.

"Blake is a lawyer. He has a paper drawn up for you to sign giving June and me permission to adopt Cathy and Max," said Jason.

"Let me see it," said Amelia reaching for the paper. She read it over and then took the pen and started to sign it.

"Hold on just a minute," said Blake. "Let me see if the

nursing home has a notary to witness your signature. I'll be right back."

Blake went out the door and Rafe and Jason turned their attention back to Amelia.

"I'm going to check and see if I can get you transferred to a nursing home in Morristown," said Rafe. "You would be close enough for us to check on you."

Amelia smiled and patted his hand. "It's a nice idea," she said. "But it is too late. I know I don't have much longer. You all will take care of Cathy and Max, won't you?" she asked.

"They are family. June and Jason already love them both and Cathy can hardly stand for June to be out of her site. I promise you they will be very well taken care of," said Rafe.

"Yes, they will," agreed Jason.

Blake returned with the notary and Amelia signed the paper and it was notarized.

After the notary left, Amelia sighed. She looked around at the men surrounding her bed and smiled.

"Thank you all for taking such care to break this bad news gently and for assuring me of my grandchildren's future, but I am very tired now and I need to rest."

Rafe leaned in and kissed her on her forehead. "Good night, Aunt Amelia," he said.

Jason leaned in and kissed her forehead, also. "I'm glad we got to meet you, Aunt Amelia," he said.

Blake offered her his hand and gave her hand a gentle squeeze.

"It was nice to meet you, Ma'am," he said.

"If you need anything, I will leave my number with the desk, you have them call me," said Rafe.

"I will," said Amelia tearfully.

The men left her room and stopped by the desk to leave a phone number for them to be called if Amelia needed them.

They went outside and started the journey home.

"I hate to leave her there all alone," said Jason.

"I know," agreed Rafe. "I'll get Mom to see if she can get her to move to Morristown."

Blake and Jason both nodded their agreement to this idea.

CHAPTER 12

*T*hey arrived back in Morristown to a warm welcome. Jason had already called June and told her he had the paper signed for them to adopt the children. June was so excited she could hardly sit still. She managed to get both children down for a nap. They had the baby monitor on with the children in the front room and all of them were sitting on the porch waiting for Rafe, Jason, and Blake when they drove up.

June hurried off the porch and was hugging Jason as soon as he could get out of the car. Everyone was smiling at her excitement.

"How was Amelia?" asked Madeline, as soon as Rafe and Blake were on the porch and Dora had hugged Rafe.

"She seemed very weak," said Rafe. "I tried to convince her to be moved here to Morristown so she would be closer, but she said she did not have much longer and she did not think it would be worth the bother."

"Maybe, I can go and see her. I don't know her very well. Amos and I had only just gotten married when she ran away. I wish she had gotten in touch with us. I know Amos missed his big sister," Madeline ended with a sigh.

"I was hoping maybe you could talk her into moving," said Rafe with a grin. He was sitting in a swing with Dora close and his arm around her.

"I can try," said Madeline with a grin.

"Well," said Blake rising. "I think I will get back to town and see about filing for the adoption. I also told Chief Welldon I would let him know how things went. Can I get a ride back to town?"

"Sure," said Liam rising from a swing with his arm around Maddie. "Maddie and I will drive you in. I think I would like to take another look around the school and gym, just to be sure there are no more surprises." Everyone laughed, but Liam looked serious.

"Thanks for all of your help," said Jason rising to shake Blake's hand.

"We are family, said Blake. "Call me if you have any questions."

The baby started fretting and June and Jason hurried inside to check on him. Liam, Maddie, and Blake left for town after a round of goodbyes and instructions from Madeline to pick up more milk.

The rest of the group started moving back inside, one by one. Madeline headed for the kitchen to see about getting food warmed up to eat. Meg followed her into the kitchen. Anna claimed her favorite seat, the bench in front of the window. Jason and June took Max to get his diaper changed and a bottle. Cathy was still sleeping on the love seat.

Lars sat down in front of the coffee table. He opened the sliding door and took out a box of Lego pieces. He and Dede had played with them for years. He started taking pieces out and fitting them together.

Cathy woke up and lay there for a few minutes watching Lars put pieces together. She finally eased off the couch and went over to where Lars was working and stood watching him. Lars smiled at her and offered her a piece.

"Do you want to help put them together?" he asked.

Cathy nodded and accepted the piece.

Lars took another piece and showed her how they fit together.

Cathy managed to get another piece to fit. She looked up at Lars and smiled. Lars smiled back at her.

"You did well," he said and handed her some more pieces.

Dora and Rafe had entered, and had been watching Lars with Cathy. Dora smiled at Rafe. She was so proud of Lars. He was a lot like Rafe. He was going to be a very loving young man. She was privileged to be his mother, she thought.

Rafe was happy watching Lars. He was proud of the way both of their children were growing up. He was looking forward to having the new baby around. Rafe reached over and laid his hand on Dora's baby bump. Dora smiled and laid her hand on top of his.

Liam and Maddie returned from dropping Blake off and looking around Maddie and June's school. After Liam took the requested milk to the kitchen, they took a seat on the abandoned love seat. Maddie leaned back into Liam's arms and watched Lars with Cathy. Cathy watched Lars' every move very closely.

Maddie stirred and gave Liam a quick kiss. She and Liam had been watching Lars with Cathy, for a while. She was happy to see Cathy interacting with Lars.

"I need to go help your mom," Maddie told Liam.

"Yes, so do I," said Dora.

She and Maddie both eased out of their love's arms and headed for the kitchen.

"Need some help?" asked Maddie as they entered the kitchen.

"It is almost ready. We already had the table set. All I had to do was get the food on the table. It was in the warmer," said Madeline. "You can call everyone to the table."

Maddie headed for the front room to announce it was time to eat. Dede was seated with Lars and Cathy, helping to build with the toys.

"Hey," said Maddie. "Where did you come from?"

"I was at dance class," said Dede. "A friend dropped me off."

"Okay, everyone, food is on the table," said Maddie.

They all departed for the dining room. Lars reached out a hand to Cathy for her to come with them. Cathy took his hand shyly and let him lead her in to eat. June and Jason were already in the dining room. They had looked in on Cathy earlier and seen her playing with Lars, so he decided not to disturb them. They had a booster seat prepared for Cathy so she could reach the table. June was holding Max and had some baby food prepared for him.

Lars helped Cathy into her seat and took the seat next to her. When they were all seated, they bowed their heads for Rafe to say the blessing. Then, they started passing food around. Each time a bowl came to Lars, he asked Cathy if she wanted some. If she said no, he passed it on. If she said yes, he gave her small servings. He did not want to overwhelm her with too much food.

Every one watched his actions with pride. He was so gentle with the little girl. She was getting over her shyness and smiling more.

They were a big happy bunch, laughing, talking, and interacting with each other. June had even managed to get Max to eat a small amount of baby food.

They had finished their meal and started cleaning the table, when Jason got a call from Blake.

"Hello," said Jason.

"Hello," said Blake. "I managed to get you and June a hearing with the judge about the adoption. It is in the morning at ten."

"Thanks, Blake. We will be there. Are you going with us?"

"Yes, I will be there. Don't worry, everything is going to be alright," said Blake.

"Thanks, we will see you in the morning."

Jason hung up the phone and turned to June.

"We have a hearing with the judge in the morning at ten," he said.

"Alright," said Madeline. "Meg can watch the children and the rest of us will go to the hearing."

"The judge only asked for me and June," said Jason.

"I know," said Madeline, "I want him to know we all will be here for those kids, the more people behind you the better."

Jason went over and gave her a hug.

"Thanks, Mom, you are the best," said Jason.

"I am just looking out for my family," said Madeline.

June came over and hugged her, too.

"I have managed to get myself a wonderful family," she said.

Madeline hugged her back.

"We are very happy to have you as part of our family. You make my son very happy," she said.

Maddie and Meg finished clearing the table and loaded the dish washer. Everyone else had gone back to the living room. Lars showed Cathy how to pick up the toys they had been playing with and put them away. After they had put everything away, Cathy looked at Lars and grinned when he told her she had done well.

"We need to get going," said Rafe, pulling Dora to her feet.

Cathy looked like she was losing her best friend when she realized Lars was leaving. Lars got down on his knees in front of her and gave her a hug.

"I have to go. I have school tomorrow, but I will see you tomorrow evening, okay," he said.

Cathy looked at him seriously for a moment, then, she nodded. Lars gave her another hug and got up to go.

Jason came over and picked up Cathy and sat down next to June on the couch. June was holding Max. Jason held Cathy close and started teasing Max. When Max started making faces, Cathy laughed. June and Jason looked at each other, startled. It was the first time they had heard Cathy laugh. They smiled at each other with satisfaction. It was a good first step. Given time, she would be alright.

CHAPTER 13

*T*hey met Blake outside the judge's chambers the next morning. He looked amused to see such a large crowd, but he did not say anything. He led the way in and motioned for everyone to take a seat. The judge was not there yet. June and Jason clutched hands. This was a nerve-racking ordeal for them. Their whole lives depended on the judge's decision. Even though everyone told them not to worry, they could not help being apprehensive.

Blake stood up when the judge entered, so everyone else stood, also.

The judge smiled at them and made a motion with his hand. "It is nice to see you, Mrs. Haggerty. You may all be seated. This is an informal hearing," said the judge.

Madeline smiled and nodded.

"I have studied the adoption request. I see no reason why Jason and June shouldn't adopt these two minor children," said the judge.

Just as everyone drew a sigh of relief, the Judge continued. "The only problem is the request is for Jason and his wife

June. I cannot sign the paper until you are married. I see you are engaged. When are you getting married?"

"The wedding is being planned. It won't be for a couple more weeks," said Jason.

"Do you want to wait and come back after the wedding to complete the adoption?" asked the judge.

June and Jason were both shaking their heads.

"I am a qualified to marry you. You could be married now and have the bigger wedding later. Then, I could go ahead and approve the adoption," the judge proposed.

Jason looked at June and she nodded and smiled.

"We would like that very much, Your Honor," said Jason.

"I thought you might. I have already obtained a marriage license just in case. Now, if you two will just fill in the pertinent facts, we can have us a wedding," said the judge.

Blake smiled. He looked at the judge. He could see the Judge was really enjoying himself. He shook his head. It did not matter as long as the adoption papers were signed. They could let the judge enjoy his moment of fun. Blake looked over the license to be sure everything was in order. He nodded his head and Jason and June stood before the judge holding hands.

"Hold on," said Maddie coming forward. "You are not getting married without your maid of honor."

Rafe came forward to stand beside Jason. He smiled at him.

"You have to have a best man," he said.

The judge smiled and rubbed his hands together. He read off the vows and got I dos from both of them. Then, he called for the rings. Jason just happened to have them in his pocket. He slipped June's ring on her finger and handed her one to put on his finger. June took the ring and slid it onto Jason's finger.

"You may now kiss the bride," said the Judge.

Jason proceeded to do just so with pleasure.

Rafe kissed June on the cheek and shook Jason's hand. Maddie hugged them both. When everyone else started to come forward, the judge raised his hand. He handed the adoption papers to Jason and said, "Congratulations, Mr. and Mrs. Haggerty you just became parents."

"Thank you, Judge," said Jason.

"Yes, thank you, Judge," agreed June.

The Judge smiled and shook both of their hands before withdrawing.

With him gone, everyone else rushed forward to hug and congratulate Jason and June.

"Why don't we take this celebration over to the restaurant?" asked Blake.

"Just for a little while," agreed Jason and June. "We have to get home to our children." Jason and June shared another big smile and a kiss.

They all headed for the restaurant next to the jewelry store. The greeter smiled at the big happy crowd coming into her restaurant. She quickly had some tables pushed together so they could all sit together.

Maddie and Dora were busy snapping pictures with their cell phones. Anna got her phone out and started snapping, too, after she saw Maddie and Dora taking pictures. Madeline smiled happily for the camera. Jason and June were oblivious to it all. They only had eyes for each other. They held on tightly to each other's hands, and Jason kissed her every chance he got.

The waitress came over, and they ordered tea all around. They ordered a light meal, because no one was very hungry. They were too excited to eat.

July came into the restaurant for her lunch break. She saw

the big happy crowd and was surprised to see her sister in the middle of it, all wrapped up in Jason's arms. She frowned and then she noticed Blake in the crowd. He was smiling at a girl, sitting next to him, and seemed to be having as good a time as everyone else. July turned away and went to see about getting a take-out for lunch.

Blake looked up and saw July turn away and head for the counter. He excused himself to Maddie, whom he had been talking to, and headed over to speak to July.

"Hello," said Blake from behind July.

July turned, startled.

"Hello," she said smiling.

"Why don't you come over and join the crowd? You can congratulate your sister and Jason. They just got married and adopted two children," said Blake.

"They adopted two children!" said July, startled.

"Yes, come on over," said Blake. He took her hand and, ignoring the shock, led her toward their table.

"Look who I found," said Blake.

Everyone looked at him. Some were surprised to see someone looking like June. Maddie was frowning. June looked surprised. She squeezed Jason's hand and smiled at July.

"July," she said. "Why don't you join us?"

Blake pulled out a chair and seated July in it. He started introducing everyone around the table. Everyone nodded politely and said hello. July was pleased to note the girl, who Blake had been laughing with, was his sister.

"Congratulations on your marriage and the adoption," July said to June and Jason. June looked surprised. "Blake told me about it," July explained.

"Thank you," said June, smiling at Jason.

"Thank you," said Jason.

"Blake told me you were working at Dulcie's hair salon," said June. "How do you like it?"

"It has been great so far. Everyone has been very nice. I have even picked up a few repeat customers," said July.

"Why did you decide to move from Denton?" asked Jason.

"All of my family is gone from there. I knew June was going to Morristown so I decided to check it out," said July.

"How did you know I was going to Morristown?" asked June.

"Because I knew you had seen Jason in the mirror," said July.

"How did you know? I did not tell anyone. I did not even know who he was until Maddie told me," said June.

"I saw him in the mirror in the museum in Denton when you did," said July.

June gasped and looked at Maddie.

"I did not think anyone but me could see him," she said.

Maddie looked thoughtful.

"Maybe it wasn't the mirror showing him to July," said Dora. "Maybe it is a twin thing. Maybe July was only seeing what you were seeing because you two are twins."

June thought about it for a moment. "I suppose it is the only explanation," she said.

"I didn't see you in the museum," said June.

July looked guilty.

"I had seen you go in and I followed you. I was going to ask you about Mom, but you disappeared before I got a chance, and I had to go back to work," said July.

June still was not satisfied, but she let it go.

"We have to get home," she told Jason.

Jason nodded. He started to reach for the check but Rafe and Blake beat him it.

"We'll split it," said Blake, smiling at Rafe.

"Okay," said Rafe.

"It was nice to meet you, July," said Madeline as they all started to get up and prepare to leave.

Blake took July's hand and helped her up. He kept a hold of her while he and Rafe went and took care of the check. When it was paid and everyone started leaving, Blake guided her over to a single table.

"What are you doing?" asked July.

"I'm buying you lunch. You haven't had anything to eat. You have to eat before you go back to work," said Blake.

"You don't have to do that, I can just grab a sandwich," said July.

'You're already here. Why not eat?" said Blake. "You can keep me company. I find myself with an appetite."

"Okay," said July with a grin.

After they ordered a light lunch, July looked at Blake curiously.

"How did June and Jason end up adopting two children?" she asked.

"Their parents were cousins of Jason's family. They were killed in a car crash, and June and Jason wanted to take care of the children," said Blake.

July looked at Blake like she thought there might be more to the story. Then, she shrugged and let it go.

"Do you really like working at Dulcie's?' asked Blake.

"Yes, I do, everyone has been very nice and easy to get along with," said July.

"So, do you think you may make this move permanent?' asked Blake.

"I'm thinking about it," said July.

"Do you think you might like to have a meal and go to a movie with me soon?" asked Blake.

July was quiet for a minute, then, she smiled shyly at Blake.

"I think I might like to eat and see a movie with you," she said

Blake grinned and took a hold of her hand. At the familiar shock, Blake shook his head.

"Maybe we can find out why we shock each other every time we touch," he replied.

"I have never had it happen to me before," said July.

"I haven't either, but someone should be able to tell us why it is happening," Blake replied.

Blake paid the bill and walked outside with July. He still had a hold of her hand.

"I guess I have to let you get back to work," remarked Blake.

"Yes," agreed July.

They stood looking in each other's eyes. Blake leaned forward and gently placed a kiss on July's lips. When he pulled back, July sighed. Blake smiled at her.

"I'll see you, soon," he said.

"Yes," said July with a nod.

They reluctantly dropped hands and July turned and entered Dulcie's. Blake looked after her for a minute then he turned and headed for his office. He completely forgot his car, parked across from the judge's chambers.

CHAPTER 14

*J*ason and June had ridden into town with Maddie and Liam. On the way home, Maddie asked June if she was still going to be in the double wedding.

"I don't see any need for it," said June. "We are already married. If we want to renew our vows, we can do it in a few years. Right now, we want to concentrate on the children."

"Are you sure you don't want the big wedding?" asked Jason.

June rubbed her hand over his cheek.

"All I want is to be your wife, and now, I am," she said with a smile. Jason smiled back and leaned in for another kiss.

"Alright, if you don't want another wedding, we will give you a reception this weekend. Madeline and I can arrange it. It will be in the side yard next to the orchard. We can put up a tent, like we did at Rafe and Dora's wedding in Rolling Fork. I'll call Bobby and see if he can come. Jason can invite his workers to meet him. Don't worry about a thing. Madeline and I can handle everything," said Maddie.

Liam looked over at her determined expression and smiled. He reached over and squeezed her hand. Maddie's expression softened, and she smiled back at him and rubbed his hand against her cheek.

When they arrived home, Maddie hurried to tell Madeline her idea. Madeline thought it was a great idea. She began making lists and calls to get started organizing the reception. Jason and June took the children into the back yard to play for a while. Maddie carried her phone onto the porch to call Bobby. She dialed his number and sat down into the swing next to Liam and waited for an answer.

"Hello, Maddie my girl. How are you?" asked Bobby.

"I am fine, Bobby. Are you going to be busy this weekend?" asked Maddie.

"No, I am free for the next month," he replied. "Is something going on?"

"I am going to be getting married in a couple of weeks. I was going to have a double wedding with my friend, but she and her fiancée had to be married today so they could adopt a couple of recently orphaned children. So, Madeline and I are having a wedding reception this weekend for them. I was hoping you could come to it and to mine and Liam's wedding in a couple of weeks. I would really like to see you. I haven't seen you in ages."

"Sure, I would love to check up on my favorite ladies. How are your mother and Dora doing?" he asked.

"They are doing great. Mom and Dad were here to visit a couple of nights ago. Dora is happy as can be. She and Rafe are expecting," said Maddie.

"I am happy to hear it," said Bobby.

"Bobby, are you and the Highlighters still playing together?" asked Maddie.

"Yeah, we get together whenever we can," said Bobbie.

"Do you think you could get them to play at the reception? It's going to be in Morristown. We will have a tent set up and have food and drinks, nothing alcoholic." said Maddie.

"I'll check and call you back, but I'm pretty sure everyone is free," said Bobby.

"Thanks, Bobby, you are a sweetheart," said Maddie.

"Who are you marrying?" asked Bobby.

"I'm marrying Rafe's brother, Liam," said Maddie. "He's a sweetheart, too." Maddie smiled at Liam and snuggled closer to him.

"He would have to be to deserve my special girl," said Bobby.

"Let me call my guys and I'll call you back," said Bobby.

"Okay, thanks, Bobby," said Maddie as she hung up and turned to Liam for a kiss.

Liam was happy to cooperate. He pulled her closer, and the kisses deepened. After a few minutes of heavy kissing, they were interrupted by the phone ringing. Maggie leaned her head into Liam's chest and took a deep breath before she answered.

"Hello," she said.

"Hi, sweetheart, I talked to the guys and they are delighted to play for you. They are looking forward to seeing you guys," said Bobby.

Maddie perked right up. "Oh, thank you, Bobby. Tell the guys I am looking forward to catching up with them, too. See you this weekend," said Maddie.

Maddie grabbed Liam's hand and headed inside. She caught up with Madeline, Meg, and Anna, sitting at the table, making plans.

Madeline smiled at them. "The tent will be set up Friday and picked up Sunday. It will have fairy lights around it and will be wired for music. There will be a stage and dance floor, and a place for a non-alcoholic bar on one side," she said.

"Great," said Maddie. "I just talked to Bobby. He is coming and he is bringing his band, the Highlighters with him."

"Bobby and the Highlighters are going to be here!" exclaimed Meg and Anna. They jumped up and danced around the room.

Madeline laughed at their antics. "Now, all we need is a caterer and someone to hand out drinks," she said.

"Lester could handle the bar," said Maddie. "We'll call the restaurant in town about catering."

"It's all coming together nicely," said Madeline.

"How do we go about inviting everyone?' asked Maddie. "We don't have time to send out invitations."

"Jason and I can tell the guys at work tomorrow," said Liam.

"We can call the pastor and have him invite everyone in church on Wednesday night." said Meg.

"I'll call Mom and Dad and invite them, said Maddie.

"Everyone just invite whoever you think of and tell them everyone is welcome." said Madeline.

"Besides the caterer, we can set up the grill, and Rafe, Jason, and Liam can make hamburgers and hotdogs for the kids," said Madeline.

"What are we going to wear," asked Meg.

"We are going to be casual. We can wear jeans or shorts. Whatever feels comfortable," said Madeline.

Liam took Maddie's hand and leaned in close. He told her he wanted to talk to her about something on the porch. Maddie smiled and let him lead her outside.

When they were on the porch, Maddie turned and raised her face for a kiss. Liam was happy to oblige.

"This is not what I brought you out here for," said Liam while kissing her again.

"Okay," said Maddie. "I'll behave."

"Please don't," said Liam. He leaned back after another kiss. "I was thinking. It is not very practical for us to arrange all of this and just have to do it all over again in another week. Why can't we have a private wedding with just family at the church on Friday, and then the reception could be for all four of us and we wouldn't have to repeat it all?" Liam finished and waited for Maddie to speak.

Maddie looked thoughtful, then, she smiled.

"I like it," she said. "Let's see if we can do it."

They went back inside to find Madeline. She and the girls were still in the dining room.

"Liam had an idea," said Maddie. "He suggested we see if the pastor can marry us on Friday in a private ceremony, with just family, at the church. Then, the reception could be for both couples and we wouldn't have to repeat it in a week."

Madeline thought about it for a minute.

"It could work. All we would need is an extra cake and banner. Also, school is going to be out for the summer on Thursday and Dede has dance camp starting the next Monday. She would be disappointed if she couldn't go," said Madeline. "I will call Lucy and see what she says. Meg, you call the pastor and see if he is free on Friday. Liam you and Maddie talk to June and Jason and make sure they have no objections."

Every one scattered to follow her directions.

Jason and June thought it was a great idea. The pastor said the church was free on Friday, and he would be glad to marry Liam and Maddie. Lucy said she would talk to the Judge, but she thought it was a great idea. She insisted she and the Judge were going to pay half of everything. Madeline gave in gracefully. After all, everything was getting rather expensive.

They all met back in the dining room and reported mission accomplished.

"I'll call Uncle Ralph," said Maddie. "I don't have time to send him an invitation."

She took her phone and went into the front room to call him . When she came back a short time later, Maddie smiled at them all.

"Uncle Ralph has something he can't get out of this weekend, but he is sending an intern with gifts for both couples," she said smiling.

"Jason will be relieved," said Liam. They all laughed.

Maddie called Blake and filled him in. He said he would be there and asked if July had been invited.

"I don't think so. I'll ask June. She and Jason should be in soon. It's about time for the children to take a nap," said Maddie.

Jason and June entered with the children. June went to fix Max a bottle, and Jason carried Cathy over to a rocking chair and sat down with her. She was about to fall asleep. He rocked her a few minutes and then got up to give the chair to June, so she could feed Max. He lay Cathy down in the living room and turned on the baby monitor.

"Blake asked me if you invited July to your reception," said Maddie.

"No, I haven't talked to her," June replied. "If I can get one of you to keep an eye on the children, I'll get Jason to take me to town to talk to her," replied June.

"There are plenty of us here to watch two babies," said Maddie. "Don't worry."

June smiled at Maddie and went to lay Max in his crib.

Jason pulled her into his arms and kissed her when she laid Max down. June smiled at him and, putting her arms around him, kissed him back.

"Can you take me to town?" June asked Jason. "I want to talk to July," she said. Jason frowned but agreed to take her to town.

"Maddie is going to keep an eye on the children while we are gone," said June.

They went and told Maddie they were leaving and Jason guided June to his truck and helped her into the seat. When they were going, Jason looked over at June and smiled. "I'm going to have to get us a car," he remarked. "We need more room for our children."

"Our children," said June. "I like the sound of that."

Jason reached over and drew her hand under his on the wheel.

"So do I. I love you Mrs. Haggerty," he said.

"Mrs. Haggerty, I like that even more," said June.

Jason squeezed her hand as they pulled to a stop in front of Dulcie's Hair Salon.

July was at the front saying goodbye to a customer when they entered. Jason and June waited until the customer left before talking to July.

July reached under the counter and pulled out her purse and, reaching inside, drew out some folded bills. She handed the bills to Jason. He looked at them curiously. He didn't know why she was handing him money.

"The money belongs to you," said July. "When you left it on the table in Denton, I saw some guys sneaking money off tables before the waitress could get to it. I took the money and went to the bathroom. When I came out and tried to pay the waitress, she said the bill had already been paid. I realized you must have seen me take it and thought I was keeping it. I may be a flirt, but I am not a thief. I just wanted to make sure you understood what happened."

"I'm sorry. I misunderstood," said Jason putting the bills in his pocket.

July smiled. "I'm glad to have it cleared up. It has been weighing on my mind."

"The reason we came by," said June. "is that we are having a reception to celebrate our wedding on Saturday at the Haggerty home place." She handed her a piece of paper with the address. "I wanted to see if you could make it."

"Sure, I would love to come. Thanks for asking," said July.

"Good," said June smiling. "We'll see you Saturday."

They left and headed for home. June looked at Jason curiously. "Why didn't you say anything about the money," she asked.

Jason shrugged. "She's your sister. I didn't want to cause any bad feelings. Family is important to me."

"You are important to me. You can tell me anything. I will always be on your side," said June. She took Jason's hand and rubbed it against her face.

Jason stopped at their house site to see how it was coming along. June looked on in amazement. It was really beginning to look like a house.

They got out to look around. The workers greeted them and were pleased with June's comments.

"We are having a wedding reception on Saturday," said Jason. "You are all invited. Bobby and the Highlighters are going to be playing. Maybe you'll get to say hello to Bobby Larroue," he finished with a grin.

"Alright," said several of the workers. They high-fived each other excitedly. Jason and June headed on home amidst lots of excited chattering.

When they entered the house, Maddie was just coming out of the front room. She had been checking on Max and Cathy.

"They are still sleeping," she said. "Blake called. He has your marriage and adoption records. He recorded them at the court house. He saved you a copy. He said you will get a certified copy in the mail. I asked him to check with Chief Welldon about having some extra security around on Saturday. When people find out Bobby and the Highlighters are going to be here, we may have some problems."

"Why don't we see if we can borrow a couple of school buses? We can get people to park in town and ride the bus out here," said Jason.

"A great idea," said June. "I was wondering where we were going to put everyone."

"I'll call Rafe," said Jason. "He can handle the call about the buses."

Jason went onto the porch to call Rafe. June went with him. Jason pulled her close. He understood why Rafe was always holding on to Dora. After Jason explained about the buses, Rafe said he would take care of it.

"Is Maddie around?" he asked. "Dora wants to talk to her."

June went inside to get Maddie. Maddie followed her back outside and answered the phone when Jason handed it to her.

"Hello," said Maddie.

"Hi, Maddie, have you done anything about a dress, yet?" asked Dora.

"No, I haven't had time. We just decided to get married Friday," she said.

"I was wondering if you would like to borrow my dress. We are the same size and it has only been used once," said Dora.

"Are you sure?" asked Maddie.

"I'm positive. I'll bring it over and we can let you try it on and make sure it still fits," said Dora.

"Thanks, Dora, I'll take really good care of it," declared Maddie.

"I know you will. I'll be over in a bit," Dora hung up the phone.

Maddie handed the phone back to Jason. "Dora is going to lend me her wedding dress," she said.

"Wonderful!" exclaimed June giving her a hug.

"Yes, it is. I hadn't even thought about what to wear," said Maddie.

Maddie was ready when Dora arrived. They went up to Maddie's room so she could try on the dress. It fit perfectly.

"It couldn't have been better if it had been made for you," declared Madeline. She had come along to help.

"I love it. Thanks, Dora," said Maddie. She gave Dora a hug. "I promise I will take very good care of it."

"I love you and you look beautiful," said Dora.

Everything was coming together. Dora, Meg, and, Anna volunteered to decorate the church on Thursday.

Lester was delighted to be asked to tend the non-alcoholic bar. Lars asked if he could help. Rafe told him he could, but he would be keeping an eye on him.

CHAPTER 15

The Judge and Lucy arrived on Thursday. They were spending the night at Hawthorn house with Blake and Mrs. Shell. They were also going to stay over on Friday night, so they would be there for the reception on Saturday.

Meg, Anna, and June decorated the church for Maddie and Liam's wedding. They hadn't told Maddie. They wanted it to be a surprise. Rafe managed to get two buses and spread the word for everyone to park their cars on a vacant lot in town and ride out in the buses. The buses would make the trip every hour. Chief Welldon assigned a patrolman to watch the lot. They wanted to be sure no one bothered the cars.

Maddie and Dora found some semi-formal dresses for June, Dede and Dora to wear at the wedding. June was to be her matron of honor. Dora and Dede were looking forward to their bridesmaid's roles. Jason prepared himself to be Liam's best man, and Rafe and Lester were to be groomsmen.

Meg went to answer a knock on the door on Thursday. She opened the door and stood staring at a handsome young man. He stared back at her; neither of them seemed able to speak. Maddie came into the room and saw Meg at the door; Maddie came forward and looked around Meg.

"David," she said. "Hello, Did Uncle Ralph send you?"

David snapped out of his distraction and smiled at Maddie.

"Hi, Maddie, yes, the Governor sent us to deliver some wedding presents. I understand congratulations are in order."

Maddie grinned and gestured toward Meg. "Thank you, David. This is Liam's sister Meg Haggerty. Meg, David and I went to school together in Rolling Fork. David is an intern for the Governor."

"Who's us?" asked Meg.

"What?" asked David, who was staring at Meg again. "Oh, Mark Stern came along to help me carry the presents in. They are too heavy for one person."

"Hello, Mark," said Maddie, greeting the other young man standing slightly behind David. "I'm Maddie Hawthorn soon to be Haggerty."

"It's nice to meet you," said Mark, coming forward and offering his hand.

Maddie shook his hand and invited the young men inside. Liam, coming in from the back, entered the front room and looked at Maddie inquiringly. "Liam, meet David Clayton and Mark Stern. Uncle Ralph sent them with wedding presents." Liam grinned and came forward to shake their hands. "David and I went to high school together in Rolling Fork. David became a summer intern for the Governor in high school and continued after he started university. David's father is the mayor of Rolling Fork," explained Maddie.

"What are you studying at university?" asked Liam, after everyone was seated.

"I'm taking law," said David. "I have two more years."

"What about you, Mark, are you at the university?" asked Liam.

"Yes, I am taking law with David. We are roommates. David recommended me for the internship with the Governor, replied Mark.

"We need to bring in the presents," said David.

"Let me get Jason. We can help," said Liam.

"Thanks," said Mark. "They are heavy."

Liam called Jason, and they went outside to help David and Mark bring in the gifts. Maddie and Meg followed them out and stood on the porch watching as the guys went out and opened the trunk of their car.

David and Mark lifted out the first box and started walking toward the porch with it. Liam and Jason picked up the second box and followed. David and Mark eased their way up the steps and onto the porch. Meg hurried to hold the door open for them.

Liam and Jason came next with their box. They did not have to strain as much. They were used to carrying heavy loads at work. Maddie held the door open for them to enter.

Meg had taken David and Mark to the dining room so they could set the box on the table. Liam and Jason carried theirs in and set it down next to the first box.

"The Governor told us to wait until you opened them and checked them out. He wanted to make sure make sure they made the trip okay and he wanted to know if you liked them," said David.

"Where's June?' Maddie asked Jason.

"She is feeding Max," said Jason.

"We will wait until she is through," said Maddie. "Would you guys like a glass of tea?"

"Yes, please," they all replied. Maddie and Meg went to

get out the tea and glasses. They poured everyone tea and they all sat down around the table to wait on June.

"Oh, we forgot the packages in the back seat," said David. He and Mark quickly rose and hurried out. They were back in just a couple of minutes with two more packages, which they laid on the table.

Jason decided to check on June and see if she was finished feeding Max. He was back in just a few minutes with Cathy in his arms and June's hand in his.

Maddie found some scissors to cut the tape and open the packages. She cut the tape, but did not open the boxes. She was waiting for June.

"Oh my goodness," said June as she walked up to the table and looked at the large boxes.

"I have already cut the tape. Let's see what is here," said Maddie.

She and June started opening the boxes and peeling back the stuffing. There was a paper on top of the inside box.

"It says here it is a complete dinner service for twelve," said Maddie.

"Mine says the same thing," said June.

Maddie opened the inside box. On top was a beautiful, engraved, silver platter. Hers said Haggerty on top, in the middle it said, Liam & Maddie, under their names it had June 2017. June's was just like it only it had Jason & June on it.

"It is so beautiful, said Maddie showing it to Liam and Meg.

"Yes, it is," agreed June

Both girls had big smiles and there were traces of tears in their eyes. Liam and Jason gave their girls a hug. Maddie pulled back and eyed the inside box. She peeled back some more paper and gasped. The plates were white with gold trim they had the state seal in the middle of each plate. They were very delicate, but seemed sturdy at the same time. June's box had the same thing in it. Maddie put the plate and the tray back in the box and closed it up. June did hers up, too.

"You can open the other box now," said David.

Maddie looked at the other box and handed the scissors to Liam. "You open it," she said.

"Are you sure?" asked Liam.

"Yes," she said nodding.

Liam cut the tape and opened the box. There was a message just inside of the box. Liam picked it up and read it. He grinned and handed it to Maddie. "For the honeymoon," it said.

Liam opened the papers and found two crystal goblets and a bottle of champagne. "I like the way your Uncle Ralph thinks," said Liam.

"I agree," said Jason, who had an identical gift for him and June.

Maddie looked at David and Mark, who both had huge grin on their faces. "You can tell Uncle Ralph his gift is loved, and we will put it to good use. I will also be sending him a thank you note."

"From us, too, Jason and I love it," agreed June.

"I'll give him your messages," said David. "Mark and I need to get started back."

"We would love to have you stay for the party," said Maddie.

"We can't. The Governor told us to come straight back," said David. They headed for the front porch. Meg followed closely behind David. When they were on the porch, David turned to Meg. "Would it be okay if I called you sometime?" he asked.

"I would like that," said Meg. "She took out her phone

and handed it to him to put his number in. Then, she called his number so it would be in his phone.

David smiled and Meg smiled back. He took her hand and squeezed it gently.

"I'll call," he promised. He and Mark got in their car and, with a wave, they were gone. Meg let out a big sigh and sat down in a swing as everyone else went back inside.

"You're going to have to have your workers build us a nice big China cabinet to display those dishes in," June said to Jason.

Jason smiled and hugged her.

"I'll make it a top priority, just as soon as I get us a bedroom and a nursery," he promised with a kiss.

Maddie looked at Liam.

"I know," he said. We will worry about it later, when we build our house."

Maddie smiled and snuggled up to him for a kiss.

Rafe and Dora came in, followed by Dede and Lars.

"Uncle Ralph's wedding presents are on the table. Take a look, but don't get any ideas about the champagne, I have plans for it," said Maddie.

Maddie and Liam followed them into the dining room to show them their gifts. Jason and June ignored them and stayed on the sofa.

"Oh. They are beautiful!" exclaimed Dora.

"Very nice," agreed Rafe.

"Are you all set for tomorrow?" asked Dora.

"I can't think of anything else we need to do. I think we have everything arranged for Saturday, too. Now, we just have to enjoy ourselves," said Maddie.

"Trust me, there are always last-minute things to take care of," said Dora.

"I will leave the last-minute details to Mom and Madeline," declared Maddie.

Dede and Lars headed out to the back yard. They were at home here because they had spent a lot of time at the home place.

"Have you heard if Rena and her family are coming?" Maddie asked Dora

"They are coming tonight. They are going to stay at Hawthorn house with Blake, Mom and Dad," said Dora.

"We are going to have a lot of children running around here playing on Saturday," said Maddie.

"Yes, we are," agreed Rafe. "I decided to set up a bounce house for the kids. There is also going to be a water slide."

"Has anyone arranged to bring Uncle Albert and Aunt Mary to the party?" asked Maddie.

"Yes, it's all taken care of. Harry and Ruby are going to drive them over when they come. They have a van and can fit the wheelchair in it," said Liam.

"I can't think of anything else. Let's go on the porch and make out like June and Jason," Maddie told Liam.

Liam grabbed her hand and started out. He was all for her idea.

Rafe and Dora smiled at their enthusiasm and decided to do a little smooching of their own.

The next day everything went as planned. Maddie got teary eyed when she saw how they had decorated the church. The Judge escorted her down the aisle, and when the preacher asked who escorts Maddie forward into her future life, he proudly said, "Her Father does." Maddie had asked the preacher to modify the question, and he agreed. He thought it was a fine idea. The ceremony was longer than June and Jason's had been, but Maddie did not mind as long as Liam and she belonged to each other. They said their I dos and exchanged rings and a long kiss.

When they started to walk back down the aisle, Maddie looked up and saw Bobby in the audience. He was grinning at her. She stopped beside his aisle and hugged him.

"I did not think you would be here until tomorrow," she said.

"I couldn't miss seeing my special girl getting married," declared Bobby. "Ah, sweetheart, you look beautiful."

"Thank you," said Maddie, hugging him again.

Bobby reached over to shake Liam's hand. You are getting a very special girl," said Bobby.

"I know," said Liam, gazing at Maddie and smiling.

"Are the Highlighters with you?" asked Maddie.

"No, I came early for your wedding. They will be here tomorrow," said Bobby.

"We will see you at Blake's," said Maddie.

"Yes, I'll be there. Blake is letting me stay in his garage apartment for tonight," said Bobby.

Maddie gave Bobby one more hug and turned to Liam to leave the church.

They went to Hawthorn house where Blake had set up a short celebration. Everyone else followed them there. Blake had picked up July and had brought her to the wedding, and now he was taking her on to his house for the celebration. Rena and her family were there, and Maddie hugged Sissy and Adam and told them she missed them. She shook hands with Stan, Rena's husband and thanked him for coming. She hugged Rena and looked in surprise at her new baby bump. Rena just grinned at her and looked very happy. Maddie was happy for her.

After champagne was served for the adults and juice for

the younger ones, the Judge stood and proposed a toast to Maddie and Liam.

"We have a wedding gift for you and Liam and for June and Jason. I talked to Blake's Godmother. She has a villa in Naples. She and her husband are not using it at this time, but they have a housekeeper and a maid. It also has a private beach. There are some beautiful gardens around the villa. She has agreed to let you all stay there for a week, starting Monday."

He paused while both couples gave excited gasps.

"Bobby agreed to fly you there and back in his private jet, and Lucy and I have rented a limo to pick you up at the airport and to be at your disposal for sightseeing while you are there. It will also deliver you back at the airport for your trip home."

He looked at Jason and June. "Your children will be fine. There are plenty of people to look after them for a week," he declared.

Maddie jumped up to run around hugging her dad, her mom, and Bobby, thanking them all. June followed her example, and Jason and Liam shook hands with everyone, except Lucy. Her, they hugged. Everyone was so excited. The party had really started with a bang.

Jason and June left early to go and check on Cathy and Max. The rest of the group lingered for a while, just talking and catching up on each other's lives. After a while, Madeline decided it was time to go and see if everything had been set up for their party the next day. Liam and Maddie decided to go when she did. They said goodnight to everyone with assurances of seeing them the next day. Maddie gave her dad and mom extra hugs thanking them for the trip. She stopped at Bobby and hugged him also.

"Thank you, Bobby, I love the trip and everyone is excited

to hear the guys and you play," said Maddie. Liam smiled and agreed. He was staying close to Maddie.

"You are welcome, Maddie. I am glad your dad thought of it," said Bobby. He grinned at Liam and reached to shake his hand. "I'll see you both tomorrow."

After they left, Blake went to take July home, and Lucy and the Judge settled back for a nice visit with Bobby. Rena and her family decided it was time to retire. It had been a long day for them.

Everything at Haggerty house was in order. The tent was set up as was the jump house and water slide. Everything looked beautiful. Maddie gazed around with awe. The twinkling lights looked like stars, shining just for them. Jason and June came out and stood gazing around with them.

"This town will be talking about this party for years to come," said Jason, with a smile.

The others smiled and agreed.

"Well," said Maddie. "The fortune teller was right. She said to expect unexpected happenings from unexpected directions. We have had plenty of those."

"She also said we would win in the end," said June. "I am so glad our love was the winner."

She and Maddie both turned into the arms of their husbands for kisses. Both Jason and Liam were happy to give them, for they agreed wholeheartedly.

ABOUT THE AUTHOR

With five children, ten grandchildren and six great-grandchildren I have a very busy life, but reading and writing have always been a very large and enjoyable part of my life. I have been writing since I was very young. I kept notebooks, with my stories in them, private. I didn't share them with anyone. They were all hand-written because I was unable to type. We lived in the country and I had to do most of my writing at night. My days were busy helping with my brothers and sister. I also helped Mom with the garden and canning food for our family. Even though I was tired, I still managed to get my thoughts down on paper at night.

When I married and began raising my family, I continued writing my stories while helping my children through school and into their own lives and families. My sister was the only one to read my stories. She was very encouraging. When my youngest daughter started college, I decided to go to college myself. I had taken my GED at an earlier date and only had to take a class to pass my college entrance tests. I passed with flying colors and even managed to get a partial scholarship. I took computer classes to learn typing. The English Language and Literature classes helped me to polish my stories.

I found public speaking was not for me. I was much more comfortable with the written word, but researching and writing the speeches was helpful. I could use information to build a story. I still managed to put my own spin on the essays.

I finished college with an associate degree and a 3.4 GPA. I had several awards including President's list, Dean's list, and Faculty list. The school experience helped me gain more confidence in my writing. I want to thank my English teacher in college for giving me more confidence in my writing by telling me that I had a good imagination. She said I told an interesting story. My daughter, who is a very good writer and has books of her own published, convinced me to have some of my stories published. She had them published for me. The first time I held one of my books in my hands and looked at my name on it as author, I was so proud. They were very well received. This was encouragement enough to convince me to continue writing and publishing. I have been building my library of books written by Betty McLain since then. I also wrote and illustrated several children's books.

Being able to type my stories opened up a whole new world for me. Having access to a computer helped me to look up anything I needed to know and expanded my ability to keep writing my books. Joining Facebook and making friends all over the world expanded my outlook considerably. I was able to understand many different lifestyles and incorporate them in my ideas.

I have heard the saying, watch out what you say and don't make the writer mad, you may end up in a book being eliminated. It is true. All of life is there to stimulate your imagination. It is fun to sit and think about how a thought can be changed to develop a story, and to watch the story develop and come alive in your mind. When I get started, the stories almost write themselves, I just have to get all of it down as I think it before it is gone.

I love knowing the stories I have written are being read and enjoyed by others. It is awe inspiring to look at the books and think I wrote that.

I look forward to many more years of putting my stories out there and hope the people reading my books are looking forward to reading them as much.

CPSIA information can be obtained
at www.ICGtesting.com
Printed in the USA
LVHW080429120121
676231LV00011B/603/J